S0-CSY-129

JAN 2024

It's Showtime, KAVI

VARSHA BAJAJ

American Girl®

For Karishma and all the
amazing desi girls
—V.B.

Table of Contents

Happy Birthday to Me!

Chapter 1

On my twelfth birthday, I skipped downstairs singing *"Happy birthday to me!"* The staircase landing had the best acoustics in our house, so I paused there and finished the last *"meee!"* like an opera diva. Then I went to the keyboard and played a few bars of "Happy Birthday" while Scamper lay at my feet, looking up at me as if he wanted to sing along. My mother and grandmother applauded.

"Happy birthday, Pookie," Mom said, giving me a one-armed hug. In her other hand she held a coffee mug with a picture of my little brother Rishi and me. She was wearing makeup and a dress because she was off to a job interview.

"Thanks, Mom," I said, as Rishi, who's eight, came racing into the room.

"Happy birthday, Didi!" he said, hugging me. *Didi* means "big sister" in Hindi.

Mom picked up her purse. "Sorry, I've got to rush," she said. "Don't want to miss the train. We'll celebrate at your birthday picnic this evening!"

"Go, go," said Dadima, waving Mom away. Dadima

1

is my dad's mother. (That's what *dadima* means in Hindi.)
Today was a teacher training day, which meant no school,
so Dadima had come over to watch Rishi and me while Dad
was at work and Mom went to her interview.

Rishi went back to playing outside, leaving Dadima and
me to the important business of baking a cookie cake—
that's a gigantic cookie with "Happy Birthday" written on
it in icing. Dadima made the best cookies, and I liked them
even better than cakes.

While Dadima gathered the ingredients, I sang "Happy
birthday to me" once again, but this time while drumming
on the kitchen table, first with my hands and then with a
wooden spoon. The drumming gave the song a whole new
flavor—just like chocolate chips in cookies.

Then Dadima sang an old Hindi birthday song, *"Bar bar
din ye aaye,"* which means, "I hope this day comes a thousand
times." She began to dance and spin, just like I do in my
dance class. I joined her, and we whirled about the kitchen
in our bare feet. Scamper jumped around with us, as if he
wanted to dance, too.

Laughing, Dadima caught her breath and said, "Beta,
at this rate there may not be a cookie cake for the party. We
need to focus." In Hindi, *beta* means "son," but the term is
used fondly for both girls and boys.

"I agreee!" I sang, holding the note. *"Let's pretend to be in
an operaaa and siiing instead of speeeeaking!"*

Dadima laughed. With a twinkle in her eye, she sang,

2

"I have a surpriiise present for youuu! I hooope you liiike it."

She pointed to an envelope on the counter, which I hadn't noticed. Was Dadima giving me money? That wasn't like her. She typically gave presents that were hard to wrap, like sleeping bags and sleds.

"I'll let you open it when the cookie is in the oven," she said, handing me her phone with the recipe. "Right now, please read me the steps in the recipe."

Soon the kitchen was transformed into a bakery with the whir of the mixer, and the smell of butter and brown and white sugars coming together. "Beat in two large eggs one at a time," I read. "Then add vanilla."

That would take Dadima some time. I picked up my own phone and read the birthday texts from my friends.

"Sparkly birthday wishes to my bestie," Sophie wrote. She had added a GIF of elephants swaying to "Happy Birthday."

"Okay, Kavi," said Dadima. "You add the vanilla." I did, and Dadima mixed it in.

My phone pinged again. Pari had sent me links to dog videos for my birthday. Aww!

"What's next?" asked Dadima, interrupting my video.

I picked up Dadima's phone and tried to find my place in the recipe. "Okay, now for the best part," I said. "Add two cups of chocolate chips!"

"Are you sure you read that correctly?" Dadima said. "The dough doesn't look right."

"It smells perfect," I said, looking back at my phone at a cute chocolate Lab dressed up as a chocolate cake.

"Kavi," said Dadima, "what about the flour?"

"Ack!" I said, dropping my phone onto the table and peering at the recipe on Dadima's phone. "The flour! Of course, add two cups of all-purpose flour. Also one teaspoon of baking soda—did we add that yet?"

I measured out the flour and baking soda, and she beat it into the batter. Then we added the chocolate chips. As Dadima put the cookie cake into the oven, she said, "You remind me of your father when he was your age. We called him the absent-minded professor even though he was just a kid."

I couldn't imagine that. Dad was an architect now.

"Dadima," I asked, "do you think Mom will get this job?"

"I hope so," she said. "I think Neena misses working in a lab. She loved it."

My mom has a graduate degree in microbiology and worked in a lab before Rishi was born. For her sake, I hoped she'd get the job, but I'd miss having her at home for sure.

With the cookie cake in the oven, Dadima made us each a cup of sweet milky chai. She ground the cloves, cardamom, and nutmeg and added them to tea leaves steeped in boiling milk. I took a deep breath and inhaled the delicious smell.

Then Dadima handed me the envelope that had been sitting on the counter.

What could be inside? I carefully slit it open.

Inside was a homemade card, with a black witch's hat against a lime green background. As I opened the card, four tickets fell out. On the card, Dadima had written,

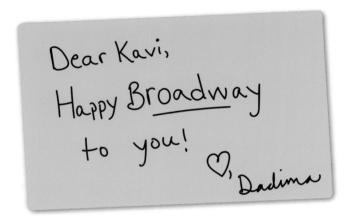

Dear Kavi,
Happy Broadway
to you!
♡, Dadima

I picked up the tickets and, in disbelief, read the top one. Then I looked across at Dadima, who was watching me intently. "You got me tickets," I whispered, "to see *Wicked* on Broadway this weekend?"

Dadima nodded, a big smile on her face, a smear of flour still on her cheek. "What do you think?" she asked.

Broadway!! We live in Metuchen, New Jersey, which is almost next door to Manhattan, but I'd never attended a Broadway show. "I've only *dreamed* of going to Broadway my whole life!" I exclaimed. "Thank you!" Then I thought of something. "Dadima, aren't Broadway tickets expensive?"

"They are," she said, "but it's a treat for my special grand-daughter. You can bring Pari and Sophie. I know you like to do everything with them. Their parents said they can go."

Happy Birthday to Me!

I jumped up. *"We're going to see **Wicked**! On Broad-waaay!"* I sang, waving the tickets around. "I can't wait!"

Dadima smiled and shook her head as I danced around the kitchen with Scamper. "Stay focused, Kavi," she said. "Don't lose the tickets!"

I went upstairs to my room. Carefully, I tacked the envelope on my bulletin board where it wouldn't get lost in my messy room. On my desk just below, my little elephant seemed to look up at me. I had named her Hattie because it sounds like the Hindi word for elephant, *haathi*. She had come all the way from India, just like Dadima. I picked her up and whispered, "Hattie, I'm the luckiest girl in the world!"

A few hours later I was helping Dadima pack the cookie cake and drinks in a picnic basket when Mom entered the kitchen with a triumphant grin and a bag of sub sandwiches.

"How did the interview go?" Dad asked her. He'd come home a few minutes earlier with hot, fresh *samosas* from my favorite shop in Edison, near where he worked.

"Great! I think I did well." Mom raised her crossed fingers. "I'll know soon if I got the job."

As we packed a blanket and silverware in the picnic basket, my best friends, Pari and Sophie, arrived.

"You'll never believe what my dadima gave me for my birthday," I told them as we climbed into Mom's car. Rishi and Dadima were riding with Dad.

"Voice lessons?" said Sophie. She knew I wanted them in addition to dance lessons.

"UGG boots?" Pari guessed. She knew I wanted some.

"Nope and nope," I said. I did a drum roll with my hands on the armrest of the car, then shouted, "She gave me tickets to see *Wicked* on Broadway—with both of you, this Sunday!"

Pari and Sophie rewarded me with stunned looks and then screams as I showed them a picture of the tickets.

Mom smiled as she popped the *Wicked* soundtrack in the CD player. (Yes, my mom still has a CD player in her car.) Clearly, Mom had known to be prepared with the CD! That was her birthday gift. Pari, Sophie, and I bounced in our seats and sang along with the music.

Soon we were cruising on the tree-lined road that led to Princeton University. A few of the trees were beginning to change colors. I always felt as if my birthday, September 30, was the start of fall.

We parked and met up with Dad, Dadima, and Rishi. As we spread our picnic blanket on the grass and looked up at the beautiful old stone buildings around us, Pari sighed. "I'd love to go to school here! I sure hope I get in."

"If you have a goal and a dream, you can work hard and get there," said Dad. "Right, Kavi?"

I nodded. "We're all taking the hard math, science, and language classes," I said. "So we can take the advanced classes in high school. That will help."

"As long as we get good grades in those classes," said Pari.

"Did you know Michelle Obama attended Princeton?" asked Sophie.

"Whoa," said Rishi. "You *really* need to have smartbrainitis to go here." Rishi was the future doctor of our family, eager to diagnose all ailments.

Sophie bit into a samosa. "Mmm, I love these!" she exclaimed, her mouth full of pastry with spicy potato-and-pea filling.

"Oooh, samosas! Pass those my way, please," said Pari.

After the meal, we all headed to my favorite place for ice cream. We were stuffed with sub sandwiches, samosas, and cookie cake, but I had to get a scoop of ice cream from my favorite shop whenever I came to Princeton. Today, in honor of the witch in *Wicked*, I got green ice cream—pistachio. Pari got blue moon, Sophie got cookies and cream, and Rishi got bubblegum. Mom and Dad said they were too full for ice cream, but Dadima got mango even though she was full too—because, she said, the mango ice cream at this shop reminds her of the mango ice cream in India. Dadima is picky about her mango flavors.

"What'll you wear to *Wicked*?" Sophie asked me as we licked our cones.

I looked at my green ice cream cone. "Maybe black and green, for the wicked witch. Only I don't have a black dress."

"You have a black skirt," said Pari, "and I've got a black top you can borrow."

"Perfect. I'll add my green belt," I said, "and my green earrings."

"My grandmother's prom dress from the fifties looks like Glinda's dress," said Sophie. "Think I should wear it?"

"Definitely," Pari and I said together. "Go for it!"

The day ended with a video call from my cousins in New Delhi, which is in India. They sang the same Hindi version of "Happy Birthday" that Dadima had. Then we all talked over each other while Scamper raced around with excitement.

As I got ready for bed, I felt completely happy. It had been such a fun evening. Tomorrow was Saturday. And on Sunday, I was going to Broadway!

It was the perfect birthday, and I had the feeling being twelve was going to be great. Maybe even the best year of my life.

Broadway, Here I Come!
Chapter 2

On Sunday right after lunch, Dadima, Pari, Sophie, and I walked to the train station and boarded a train for Manhattan. My heart pounded in rhythm with the clackety-clack of the wheels. Broadway, here I come!

After we got off the train, we walked to Times Square and turned down Broadway. We were surrounded by billboards and signs, each one advertising a different show. *Someday, I'll see all these shows*, I promised myself as we reached our theater. The marquee showed Elphaba, the green witch, with her pointy witch hat pulled over her eyes. Her green face glowed with a mysterious smile as Glinda whispered in her ear. The marquee read, "Brains, Heart, Courage."

Pari pinched me. "Can you believe we're actually here?"

I pinched Sophie and Pari. "We are! Thank you, Dadima!"

Sophie threw her arms in the air. "We're going to a Broadway show!"

I looked around at all the people entering the theater

11

with us. Some wore outfits inspired by characters in the show, like Sophie and me. Others were dressed in stylish outfits for an afternoon at the theater. The excitement in the crowd was electric.

"Dadima, your silk sari shimmers under the lights," I said, admiring it. "You've lived in America for fifty years! Why do you always wear a sari when you want to dress up?"

"I love getting dressed up in a sari," Dadima said. "Saris remind me of my Indian heritage, and they're beautiful, don't you think?" I nodded and linked my arm with hers, and the four of us made our way to our seats.

Broadway, Here I Come!

Soon, we were listening to the songs from my CD, performed live onstage! I already knew some of them. When Glinda sang, "Popular," I sang along under my breath, wishing I could rise from my seat and move with the music.

The actors were amazing singers and dancers, and the sets were beautiful, but the part I loved most was the story of Elphaba and Glinda, two girls who started out as friends but became enemies. As the second act began, I hoped with all my heart that they would become friends again. I squeezed Pari's and Sophie's hands. I couldn't imagine not being friends with them. At the end, when Elphaba and Glinda reunited, I hugged my friends and sighed with happiness.

The whole show was a beautiful fantasy, but it had also made me think. The story it told was about using the traits you're born with, for good or for bad. And sometimes, the show seemed to say, good and bad are hard to tell apart.

The audience gave a standing ovation as the actors took their bows. How thrilling it must be, I thought, to perform in a show like this!

Suddenly I knew it was exactly what I wanted to do, if I ever got the chance. Our school put on a musical every spring. Maybe I could be in it!

Monday morning, as I arrived at school, I saw a group of kids gathered at the far end of the seventh-grade corridor. Curious, I walked over. They were looking at a poster on the wall that said:

With eager eyes, I read the poster. Students had to be in good academic standing to participate. The live performance would be in the middle of November, in about six weeks.

My brain began to spark with excitement. Last night, after seeing *Wicked*, I'd dreamed that I was in the play, singing and dancing onstage while the audience cheered. The feeling was like flying and being admired and famous all rolled into one. What could be better than that?

Finally, Dadima picked up and said, "Hello? Kavi?"

The words tumbled out of my mouth. Flustered and rattled, I barely made sense, but she understood me anyway. I tried to eat my breakfast while I waited for her to arrive, but I'd lost my appetite. Dadima lived only a few miles away, yet she seemed to be taking forever. Was I going to be late for school?

When her car finally pulled up, I flew out the door and into the front seat. Dadima had thrown a coat over her pajamas, and she still wore her house slippers. Sheepishly, I knew she must have rushed, like a swirly wind.

The drive to school was silent. As she pulled up in front of the school, Dadima said quietly, "We don't need to tell your mom. It would only worry her and add to her stress. I'm sure it won't happen again." I nodded gratefully and got out of the car.

I took a deep breath under the huge old oak tree outside the auditorium and then entered the school. The hallway was empty. My footsteps echoed in the silence, and my heart pounded. I knew I needed to report to the front office.

The office lady frowned and handed me a yellow slip of paper for my parents to sign.

I'd received my first tardy.

Flushed, I tried to calm my racing thoughts as I found my class and took my seat. Sophie looked at me with concern. Mrs. Roberts was explaining some equations on the board with positive and negative numbers, but I couldn't

focus on what she was saying. *What will happen if I don't return the tardy slip?* I wondered. Would the school call my parents to tell them? I hated the thought of disappointing my mother on the first day of her new job.

Outside the classroom window, movement caught my eye. Two squirrels were scurrying up and down the big oak tree. They chased each other, their tails all fluffed up. They were so cute!

A kick on the back of my chair startled me. Sophie hissed, "Kavi!" Mrs. Roberts repeated her question. "Kavi, which of these equations has a product that is negative?"

Quickly, I thought back to what the teacher had taught us, about how multiplying two negative numbers makes a positive. I scanned the board. "Um, the first and the fourth ones?" I asked.

Mrs. Roberts nodded, and I sank back in my seat with relief.

The school day seemed to stretch to eternity. I vowed I'd never miss the bus or be tardy again. But when I got home, I couldn't find my science textbook, and I needed it to do my homework. Had I left it somewhere at school?

The last time I forgot a textbook, Mom suggested I call Pari and then drove me to her house so I could borrow the book and do my homework. Today Mom wasn't home to drive me anywhere. And I couldn't call on Dadima twice in one day. But I could walk to Sophie's house, so I called her.

"I'm so sorry, Kavi," said Sophie. "I finished the worksheet in class, so I didn't bring the textbook home."

Darn. If only I'd done that!

Seeing me lost in thought, Rishi stuck the end of his stethoscope on my head and said, "Didi, you have a bad case of daydreamitis."

I shrugged him off. "Rishi, go away. You're not a doctor, and that's not even a real diagnosis. Leave me alone." He looked surprised and hurt at my sharp tone and ran off with Scamper.

Since I couldn't do my homework, I wandered to the keyboard and decided to practice. I played the first chord and felt lighter as I relaxed into the music. Soon, the perfect acoustic spot on the staircase called to me. I left the keyboard, stood on the landing, and belted out a song from *Wicked*, adding the spin step I'd seen the actors do in the show.

"Don't you have homework?" Rishi asked.

"I forgot my textbook," I said, doing another dance step.

"Didi," said Rishi, shaking his head, "you've got a bad case of Broadwayitis."

Maybe Rishi was right. A diagnosis like that could explain a lot!

When Mom and Dad came home, Mom was full of stories about her new lab. She told us about the coworker who sang to himself as he worked, and the colleague who'd brought the most delicious coffee cake to share, and how cold the lab was. "I'll bring a cardigan to work tomorrow," she said cheerfully. Mom looked around the table at us and said, "Hope things here went off without a hitch."

"As far as I know they did," said Dad. "I didn't get any calls."

I almost blurted out the truth, but I said nothing. I'd never felt so guilty.

Rishi piped up, "Kavi has a bad case of—"

Before he could complete the sentence, I said loudly, "Everything went fine, Mom," I said. "You can count on us."

As we got up to clear our plates, I whispered, "Rishi," and signaled, *Zip it.*

Rishi hissed back, "Do you have Pinocchioitis? That's when someone's nose grows when they lie."

"I just don't want to worry Mom," I told him. "She doesn't need to know every single thing I do." Silently, I promised myself I'd do better tomorrow.

The next day in science class, Mr. Proton greeted us with a cheery, "Good morning!"

Twice in One Day

Would it be a good morning? I didn't have my science homework done. I held my breath, hoping he wouldn't call for it.

Our science teacher's real name is Mr. Proszynski, but everyone calls him Mr. Proton because of his love of the atomic structure. He always joked, "At least I'm the positive one!"

As students began handing in their homework, good old Mr. Proton waved them away, saying, "I don't need your worksheets today. I'll check all your assignments on Friday. Please take your seats."

I exhaled with relief. Whew!

"It was hard, but I did it—and now you don't even want it?" Jake asked.

"Nope, not right now," Mr. Proton replied, handing out new worksheets. Papers rustled and the kids at the back of the room whispered. "Instead, we're having a pop quiz," he announced. Several kids groaned.

What? My stomach dropped. This was like a roller coaster of feelings, relief followed by panic.

"If you did your homework, you'll have no problem with the quiz. It'll be easy peasy," said Mr. Proton. The groans got louder.

"If you didn't do your homework," Mr. Proton continued, "then you may find this quiz quite challenging."

All I could hear was the rush of *Noooooooooooooooooo!* in my mind. This couldn't be happening!

I picked up the quiz and read the questions. The quiz was multiple-choice, with three possible answers for each question. The choices were tricky: not just straightforward A, B, or C, but also *A and B*. Or *A and sometimes B, but never C*. Ugh!

Most of my classmates were scribbling away furiously, drawing diagrams and figuring answers. I stared at my quiz in desperation. The one thing I did know is that in a multiple-choice test, I was better off making guesses, because I had a one-in-three chance of getting the right answer. I began circling answers at random. What else could I do?

After the quiz was over, Mr. Proton asked us to grade our own work as he read out the answers. Out of ten problems, I got two correct. They were lucky guesses. Then he asked us to come to his desk with our quizzes so he could grade our scores. My feet felt like lead as I dragged myself to the front of the room and handed him my quiz.

He looked at my sheet and his brows rose. "Kavi? This isn't up to your usual standard," he said, picking up a red marker and writing an F on the top of the page. He circled it, and I felt as if it covered the whole page. I'd never gotten an F before.

"You'll need to bring this back with a parent's signature," he told me. Mortified, I hurried back to my seat, hoping nobody had seen.

Later as we walked to the next class, Sophie said, "Kavi,

did you find a way to get the textbook last night? I was hoping you did."

I was too embarrassed to tell Sophie the truth, but before I could say anything, Pari exclaimed, "That quiz was tough. I can't believe I managed to get an A."

I wasn't about to tell them that I'd gotten an F. I buried my quiz with the big red F in the dark depths of my backpack. How would I get Mom and Dad to sign it without them asking questions that I didn't want to answer?

After school, Rishi had soccer practice, and I went straight upstairs to my messy room and did my homework. When I came down, Mom and Dad and Rishi were all in the kitchen. Mom had made *raajma*, which is a spicy stew of kidney beans, and Dad was making rice flavored with cumin to go with it. Rishi was peeling cucumbers for a salad.

"Ooh," I said, "I love raajma with rice."

The voice in my head said, *Just tell them everything. Get them to sign the tardy slip and the quiz with the F.* But I was terrified about what they would say. My anxiety felt like quicksand around my feet.

I slipped out of the kitchen. Across the dining room, the keyboard was calling to me. Music practice was much safer! I opened the piano bench, fished out my music, and sat down to play.

The song started slow and built to a crescendo as I sang along. Singing and playing together was hard. I focused and concentrated, which drowned out all my other worries, and I began to relax into the song, feeling my emotions flow out through the music.

When I finished the song, I heard applause, and I realized my family had come out of the kitchen to listen to me. Dad hugged me and handed me a glass of juice.

Rishi held his stethoscope to my back. "Didi, you have superstaritis, one hundred percent."

"Kavi," said Mom, "you're so talented. I'm proud of you. How was school today?"

Here was yet another chance to tell them. But I wasn't brave enough. Instead, I heard myself saying, "Fine, Mom. Just fine."

If only she knew. My half-truths and fibs were piling up like a heap of dirty laundry.

Dad raised his glass and said, "To Neena, for sailing through her first two days back at a full-time job."

Mom raised her glass to me and said, "To our superstar!"

My juice tasted like bitter medicine and sour cherries, because I had just lied to my family. I didn't deserve their praise. If they knew the truth about my day at school, they would be so disappointed!

What's Most Important
Chapter 4

A few nights later, my parents were both in the kitchen, cooking. As I was setting the table, I heard Mom say to Dad, "Remember that tomorrow is Kavi's parent-teacher conference. Can you pick me up at the train station at three o'clock, and we can drive to the school together?"

I nearly dropped all the silverware on the floor. How could I have forgotten that parent-teacher conferences were tomorrow? As we all sat down at the table, my stomach did a backflip.

"Kavi, we'll meet you at school," said Mom. "Don't take the bus home—your teachers want you there for the conference, too." She turned to my brother. "Rishi, you have soccer practice tomorrow, so I'll pick you up after practice."

Rishi nodded and began chattering about his soccer team and their new coach. I was thankful, because it meant I didn't have to say anything. All I could think about was tomorrow's conference, which I definitely didn't want to talk about.

I'd never had a problem with teacher conferences in the

past. My teachers always told my parents I was doing well, and Mom and Dad smiled with pride. Everyone was happy, and we celebrated with ice cream.

It would be different this year.

As I met my parents after school the next day, my mouth was dry. We sat across from my homeroom teacher in an empty classroom, where we would be meeting with my teachers one at a time.

My homeroom teacher began, "Seventh grade can be a challenge, so I just want to be sure that everything is okay."

"Isn't it? What do you mean?" Mom looked confused.

"Well," said the teacher, "Kavi has never been late to school before, until last week."

"Kavi was late to school?" Now Dad looked confused.

"I'm sure we sent home a tardy slip," the teacher looked at her laptop. "It looks like the slip never came back to school. Kavi? Did you get it signed?" She pulled up a copy of the yellow slip on her laptop and showed it to us.

Mom's eyes widened. "That was the date I started . . ." her voice trailed off.

"We all oversleep sometimes," said the teacher.

Mom swallowed and nodded. "It won't happen again."

As the homeroom teacher left and Mrs. Roberts came in, Mom said quietly, "Kavi, I want to hear about this when we get home."

What's Most Important

Mrs. Roberts commented that I seemed to be struggling a bit with some of the new math concepts, and my homework was sometimes incomplete.

Dad raised his eyebrows. "Kavi, feel free to ask me or Mom for help if you need it."

"The school is here to support you, too," said Mrs. Roberts. "You can always talk to your teachers or your counselor if you need extra help."

"Okay," I mumbled, wishing this was over. But I knew the worst was still to come.

Mr. Proton arrived and stated that I had a good head for science but seemed a little unfocused. He mentioned the failed science quiz.

"What?" Dad said, his voice getting squeaky. "Are you sure you aren't confusing Kavi with another student?"

"No, Mr. Sharma, I'm not. But I'm sure Kavi knows that she can improve her grades by studying," Mr. Proton said.

By this point, all I wanted was to disappear. Be teleported to another planet. Or wear Harry Potter's invisibility cloak.

"May I see the quiz?" asked Dad. He still looked skeptical, as if he didn't believe his daughter could fail a quiz.

"I sent it home with Kavi for you to sign . . ." Mr. Proton looked through a folder of papers. "Kavi, did you return the signed quiz?"

I looked down at my shoes. I couldn't bring myself to face the three pairs of eyes that were looking at me. I shook my head.

"Kavi, wait a minute," Dad said. "You hid this from us?"

I reached into the depths of my backpack and fished out the quiz, all crumpled into a ball. Dad uncreased it and looked at me as if I were an alien. Then he pulled out a pen and signed next to the big red F at the top.

I wished I didn't have a big lump in my throat and could say, "I'm sorry." But I couldn't speak. It was all I could do to not cry.

Mom reached for my hand as we walked out. Our car was parked in the shade of the big oak tree. None of us said anything as we walked to the car.

The drive home was quiet. As we entered our house, Dad put his hand on my shoulder. "Kavi, we'll talk, after Mom and I have discussed things." My parents retreated to their room.

I fled to my room. Scamper followed. Since he's the smartest dog in the world, he knew something was up.

After a bit I needed a drink of water. In the hallway, I could hear the low murmur of my parents' voices.

"Arun, do you think I shouldn't have gone back to

work?" Mom asked Dad.

"This is not your fault," he replied.

"She was doing fine when I was at home," said Mom. "She always had excellent grades in all her classes. But seventh grade *is* harder. I've heard other moms say that."

"Neena, face it, these patterns aren't new," said Dad. "You've helped her stay on top of things by giving her lots of reminders, but Kavi needs to learn how to be independent. You can't live her life for her." He went on, "Neena, I'm more worried that she deceived us. How did we get to this place where Kavi feels she can't talk to us?"

There was a long silence. I felt a single tear roll down my cheek.

"I need to pick up Rishi from soccer practice," Mom said finally. "We'll talk to her when I return."

I slipped back into my room. To distract myself, I cranked up the music for the dance Pari and I were learning for Diwali. At least I could work on our dance routine. Maybe that would cheer me up. Maybe we could even perform it in the revue!

Suddenly the words on the poster popped into my mind: to participate, students must be in *good academic standing*.

"Am I still in good academic standing?" I asked Scamper and Hattie. "Will my grades disqualify me?"

Scamp whimpered in sympathy. Hattie was silent, as usual, but her wise expression told me she understood how I was feeling.

If only I could wave a wand and go back to my birthday and then start last week over. But here I was, after dinner on the day of the parent-teacher conference, going through my homework assignments with my parents at the kitchen table.

Almost as if he was reading my thoughts, Dad took my hand and said, "We're in this together, beta. We'll figure it out."

I nodded. But really, it was easy for *him* to say. *I* was the one in a pickle, not him.

Mom gave my back an encouraging pat. "Pookie, do you think your classes are too much for you?"

I shrugged. Did I have too much? I liked all my teachers, and I wanted to be with my friends. When I put my mind to it, I could usually do the work. But sometimes it was just so hard to focus. And now that I had fallen behind, trying to catch up felt like climbing a mountain.

"Kavi is a bright girl," Dad said. "I'm sure she can handle the academics." Did he really believe that? Did I? I wanted to, but— "The revue might be too much, beta," Dad added. "I think it tipped over the apple cart."

"Will I have to quit the revue?" My question flew out into the room like a bird released from a cage.

"Your education is what's most important," said Dad. "Everything else is secondary."

Mom nodded. "Kavi, you know that, right?"

"I don't know anything," I said. Then I blurted out, "What if I'm just not as smart as the rest of you? That happens, you know."

"Kavi!" said Mom. "Don't be absurd." Mom squared her shoulders. "We just need a plan to get your schoolwork back on track."

We decided that I'd ask my teachers about extra-credit assignments to bring my grades up. Also, until the revue was done, I'd take a break from my piano lessons. After the revue, I would take a break from dance lessons, too. Once I was all caught up with schoolwork and keeping my grades up, we'd reintroduce piano and dance lessons one at a time. I could live with that.

Scamper followed me up to my room. "Scamp," I said, "I am the bad apple of this smart family. I cause Mom and Dad so much stress. I wish I was a better daughter." He tilted his head at me, perking his ears forward and gazing into my eyes. *Really? You think that?* he seemed to say. "It's just that school used to be pretty easy for me, and now it's harder," I told him. "But I can't figure out why I'm so forgetful and late all the time." Scamp licked my hand. "All I know is I really don't want to drop out of the revue. But if I don't improve my grades . . ." I didn't finish the thought. Scamp laid his head in my lap in sympathy. I hugged him, burying my face in his fur.

What if I really *wasn't* as smart as everyone thought?

That would explain a lot!

Would Pari and Sophie still want to be friends with me if I wasn't as smart?

Rishi must have overheard our conversation after dinner, because suddenly I heard him ask Mom, "Does Kavi have stupiditis?"

"Of course not!" Mom said. "What kind of question is that? You'll not use that word in this house again."

If my own brother thought I was stupid, would my friends think the same?

I texted Pari.

If I don't get into Princeton with you, would you still be my friend?

She replied,

 Don't be silly!

Just as I was trying to decide whether she meant it was silly to think I might not get into Princeton or silly to think she wouldn't be my friend if I didn't get in, my phone pinged again. It was Pari:

 I'm in!

Wait, what?

Already? So Princeton admits seventh-graders if you're really smart?

Pari was the smartest kid I knew.

She texted back.

 I mean I'll be in the revue with you!

Did she know it was the perfect way to cheer me up?
Of course she did. Because she's my friend. I replied,

Then I texted Sophie.

Pari's in!!!

Now all I had to do was get my grades up so that I'd be in good academic standing.

My phone pinged. Sophie texted back:

Yay! Hip-hop till we drop!

Distractions and Diwali

Chapter 5

The next day, when I got home after school, I retreated immediately to my room and waded through the piles of clothes on my floor until I reached my bed. I had several chapters of a book to read for English, but I didn't feel like starting it. I lay on my bed with Scamper and looked at my phone.

"Kavi," I heard Dadima call. "Come downstairs. We can read together." My parents had decided that Dadima should come over after school to take care of Rishi and me, help us with schoolwork, and stay until they got home.

I knew what she was doing. She wanted to make sure I wasn't staring out the window or at my phone instead of reading. I got out notebook paper and a marker and made a sign that said "I DON'T NEED HELP!"

I showed it to Scamper. "Think she'll get the hint?" I asked him. But before I could tape the sign onto my bedroom door, Scamper grabbed it in his mouth and chewed it up.

Smart dog.

I heard footsteps on the stairs, and Rishi poked his

head in my room. "Dadima says she is going to make *aloo parathas* for dinner, just for you." I knew how much work it took to make the delicious flatbread stuffed with spicy potatoes. Even Rishi knew. "If you don't go down and sit with her like she asked, I'd say you have rudeitis," he added.

Little brothers can be so annoying.

I grabbed my book and went downstairs. Dadima, Scamper, and I sat on the couch and read. Scamp and I snuggled under the throw. The wind whistled outside, and the rain pattered down. After a bit, Dadima got up and began to cook dinner. Soon delicious smells wafted from the kitchen.

I had to admit, it was kind of nice having her here.

In math class the next day, I smiled when I read the first few problems on the board. The night before, Dad had used a number line to help me understand positive and negative numbers, and it made sense now. I raised my hand, eager to show that I knew the answers.

Science class was another story. I tried to concentrate on the worksheet Mr. Proton had passed out, but my brain kept getting distracted by the rhythmic sound of a pencil tapping on a desk. Then there was the sound of a chair scratching the floor. I turned around. It was Jake. Now he was making popping sounds on his cheek, inside his mouth.

"Jake!" I hissed. "Please be quiet. I can't concentrate."

"I can't either," he said. "I need to move and fidget. It's just how I am."

"It's very distracting," I said and glared at him.

Later, as we walked to the next class, Jake bumped me with his elbow. "Sorry if I was distracting. I didn't mean to be. Sometimes my brain has a hard time focusing, and fidgeting helps," he explained. "Ms. González says my brain is also creative and funny, so it all balances out." Ms. González was my school counselor. I guess she was Jake's, too.

I'd always thought Jake was just being annoying on purpose. "What do you mean?" I asked him.

He shrugged. "Well, I guess it's like my brain has a different way of working," he said. Then Jake raced off with his friends, leaving me with more questions.

Is that why I was so distracted? Was it because my brain worked differently, like Jake's?

The following Friday, as Sophie and Pari and I sat down in the cafeteria for lunch, I asked them, "Do you realize that the revue is in three weeks? And we still haven't decided what we're doing."

I turned to Sophie. "Maybe you could come to our dance rehearsal tonight and learn the dance Pari and I are doing for Diwali next week."

Diwali is my favorite holiday. It celebrates the victory of good over evil and light over darkness. It lasts five days, and our relatives here in New Jersey always come over for a big dinner. We also go to the Indian Community Center for a dance show, where Pari and I and Rina Auntie's other classes perform the special dances we've prepared.

Pari looked skeptical. "Seriously, Kavi? It's taken us more than a month to learn it, and we've been taking Kathak for a year. I don't see how Sophie could learn it in three weeks."

Sophie nodded. "Pari's right. Maybe we could do a simple tap dance. I took tap in elementary school, and I still remember the basic steps."

"Ooh, I love tap!" said Pari. "I took lessons in fourth grade. I'm a little rusty, but—"

"Excuse me, but I've never taken tap dancing," I reminded them.

"How about ballet?" Pari suggested. "You took ballet with me in third grade, remember?" she said, turning to me.

I did, but then I decided to take Indian dance instead. "I wasn't that great at ballet," I reminded her.

"Maybe you would have been if you'd stayed with it," Pari pointed out.

Sophie cut in. "I don't know ballet, so forget about it. How about jazz?"

"Ooh, yes! A lot of Broadway dancing is jazz dance," I said eagerly. "And we had that jazz class the summer after fifth grade. It was only for a few months, but I loved it!"

"Me too—it was so much fun!" Sophie agreed.

"I haven't taken jazz dance," said Pari. "I want to, though. Maybe next year."

"Okay, let me get this straight," I said, pushing my cafeteria tray back and opening my planner to a blank page. On it I drew three interlinked circles and labeled each circle with one of our names. I showed them my drawing.

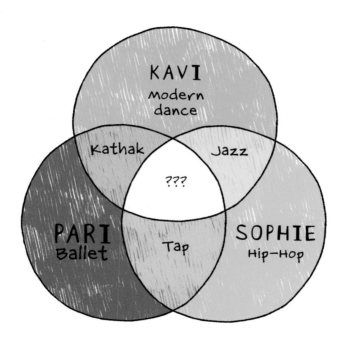

"Nice Venn diagram," said Pari.

"Thanks!" I replied.

"What goes in the middle?" asked Sophie.

"Exactly," I said. "That's the question! Whatever it is, that's what we'll do in the revue."

On Sunday, right after lunch, I put on some Indian music and began to clean my room. Once I got going, it was actually sort of fun, like an archeological excavation. I found a sweater that I'd been missing since school started, the really good earbuds that Dadima had put in my Christmas stocking, a bunch of Scamper's chew toys, some missing math homework, and—ta-da!—my missing science textbook! (Mr. Proton had kindly loaned me one, which I could now return.)

After I finished, I invited Mom up to inspect. When she saw my room, she applauded. "Bravo, Kavi!"

We went downstairs, and Mom opened a box of colorful lamps called *diyas* and some marigold garlands she had brought up from the basement to decorate the house for Diwali. Rishi and I helped her set the diyas around the dining room and on the windowsills and the mantel. We also placed them in the foyer around the *rangoli* design that we had made from colored sand. Carefully, we lit all the lamps. It was getting dark outside, and the candles looked so pretty, flickering and reflected in the windows.

Mom beamed. "Happy Diwali, Pookie!

Happy Diwali, Rishi!" she said, hugging us.

"Happy Diwali, Mom!" we replied joyfully.

At the end of the week, on Friday evening, the whole family drove over to the Indian Community Center. Rina Auntie and the other dancers were gathering in the dressing room. Pari was there too, and we helped each other get into our Kathak costumes and fasten the bells on our feet.

After our dance, we watched the older girls. Pari's sister, Priya, was one of the dancers. They were dancing to a popular Bollywood song with a beat that made my feet tap. The steps and moves were a combination of Indian dance and jazz dance and other styles, like a fusion of dance cultures. By the finale, the whole audience was clapping along. The dance beat stayed with me after the performance, and set me thinking. Was this a way our different dance styles could blend together?

That weekend, Pari and Sophie came to my house for a group study session. We were determined to learn everything we needed to know about clouds for science class. I put out snacks, according to our study group rules.

Sophie started to read aloud about the different types of cloud formations. Pari took notes as Sophie read. I was supposed to be reading along too, but my mind drifted away like a cloud on a breezy day.

The truth was, I still had Bollywood beats on the brain.

Suddenly Sophie stopped reading. "Pop quiz: Kavi, what are the long skinny clouds called?"

I blinked. "Um, skinny minis?"

"Kavi, are you reading a textbook from another planet?" Sophie asked, looking slightly exasperated.

"Have martians taken over your brain?" Pari teased.

I knew I owed Pari and Sophie an explanation.

"Sorry, sorry! I wasn't listening," I admitted. "I keep thinking about the Bollywood dance Pari's sister did for Diwali—"

"Oh, Kavi," said Sophie. "Is dancing all you ever think about?"

"Pretty much. I've had a hard time focusing on my schoolwork," I confessed. "It's like my brain is a TV that's supposed to be on the science channel—but it's stuck on the dance channel."

I thought Sophie might be annoyed with me, but all she said was, "Okay, if you like thinking about dance, then let's make up a dance for each cloud." She stood on her tiptoes and waved her hands in the air. "I'm a cirrus cloud, wispy and way up high in the sky!"

Pari jumped onto my bed and grabbed my pillows, saying, "I'm a fluffy, puffy cumulus!" She threw a pillow at me and one at Sophie. "Incoming cumulus!"

This was fun. I lay on the floor and stretched out. "Low,

flat stratus cloud here," I said, and we all collapsed in giggles. "This is the best science study session ever!"

A bit later, as we were snacking, I stared at the trail mix in my hand. It had nuts, chocolate chips, raisins, bagel chips, and pretzels, all mixed up together in one yummy snack. I jumped to my feet. "Pari, Sophie," I said, "I know what we can do for the revue."

They looked at me quizzically. "What?"

"We'll combine all our dance skills into a Bollywood dance," I said clapping my hands. "I took a Bollywood dance class last year. I bet we could learn a Bollywood routine!"

"I've heard of Bollywood, but what is it, exactly?" Sophie asked.

I went to my laptop and pulled up Priya's Bollywood routine from Friday night, which Rina Auntie had posted online, and played it for her. Halfway through the video, Sophie began to tap her foot to the beat. "Hey, I think I could learn that!" she said.

"Me too," Pari agreed. "And Priya could help us."

Together, we began copying the dancers. Sophie added a few hip-hop moves. I added a Kathak spin. Pretty soon, we'd choreographed a whole dance.

"Ready? Again—a five, six, seven, eight!" We practiced it over and over until we had it memorized. Then we fell into a heap of arms and legs, giggling and exhausted, but elated. We had our dance!

Too Much
Chapter 6

On Halloween, after an early dinner, I put on my Elphaba outfit to hand out candy with Mom, while Rishi got into his costume to go trick-or-treating around the neighborhood with Dad. Rishi wore hospital scrubs, a lab coat, surgical gloves, and a mask and had draped a stethoscope around his neck.

"Paging Dr. Sharma," I said, waving him out the door. "Candy awaits."

The next day after school, Sophie and Pari came over again so we could practice our Bollywood dance. It was raining outside, and that gave us the idea to add parasols to our act. We practiced with umbrellas. I put on Bollywood music, and Dadima and Rishi came in to watch. After we'd run through our dance a few times, Rishi and Dadima decided to join in. Soon we were all dancing together.

"You two aren't ready for the spotlight yet," I told them, laughing.

"Actually, I think they should perform in the revue with you girls," said Dad, who had just come home from work.

Sophie cracked up, but Pari's eyes widened in horror. She didn't realize Dad was joking.

"Dad! Stop! That would be terrible," I said, but I was laughing, too.

On Wednesday in homeroom, the morning announcements said that all performers in the revue should meet after school in the auditorium for a rehearsal. A real rehearsal! I couldn't wait. When the school bell finally rang, I grabbed my backpack and hurried to the auditorium.

Ms. Tucker, the English and drama teacher who was directing the revue, summoned everyone up onto the stage with her. "Students, this is our first technical rehearsal. We'll run through each act in the order I have written here," she said, waving a clipboard. "That's the order you'll be performing in the revue. You need to adjust to the stage and learn where the microphones and props are. Dancers, you should count how many steps you need to get to the center of the stage."

"It's a lot bigger than Rina Auntie's stage," Pari whispered.

While the musicians and dancers warmed up, Ms. Tucker taught the singers and comedians how to adjust the microphone height. A singer who performed in the second act, an eighth-grader named Alaina Peterson, took the microphone and sang a few bars in a pure, beautiful, clear voice. I stopped to listen, wishing I could sing as well as she did. Then Ms.

Tucker cleared the stage, and the run-through began.

Three ballet dancers took the stage. Even though they were in street clothes, I could see they had been training for years, they were so graceful. I was relieved that we had decided not to do ballet. We would have made fools of ourselves next to these dancers!

Next up was Jake and his comedy routine, which had gotten a lot better and drew laughs from the cast and crew. After Jake was the juggler, Ali. He could juggle three tennis balls really well, but when he tried to do four he kept dropping them. Five balls were hopeless. The other kids groaned and then laughed when all the balls flew out of his hands at once. Ali gave a sheepish smile, shrugged, gathered up his tennis balls and left the stage to hoots and scattered applause.

We were next.

Our music came on, and our bare feet tapped to the music until we heard the cue for us to dance out onto the stage. Since the stage was bigger than the room we had practiced in, it took us about eight extra steps to get to center stage, and by then my count was off. I was glad it was only a rehearsal.

As the beat picked up, we began our dance. Today, in place of parasols, we were using yardsticks. I remembered most of the steps, but my steps didn't seem to match Pari's and Sophie's. Was my count still off? Or were they off? I couldn't tell. We kept going anyway and were nearly to the end, in the middle of our trickiest move—spin, slide, reach, open the parasol, spin around each other—when I tripped.

My left knee hit the floor. The yardstick flew out of my hands and arced across the stage at Jake, who was sitting in the first row.

"Hey, Kavi, nice shot!" he said, ducking.

It all happened so quickly! I watched the flying yardstick in horror, missed another step, tried to recover, stubbed my toe, and landed flat on my face.

The music faded. All I could hear was my heart thudding in my ears, gasps, and then snickering and laughter once the other students saw I wasn't hurt.

Pari reached out and helped me up, and I left the stage in tears of humiliation. It felt like the worst moment of my life.

Ms. Tucker stopped me. "Kavi, are you okay?" she asked with concern.

Why did I think doing a whole new dance that we had only learned a few days ago was a good idea? "I can't do this," I blurted out.

"Kavi, dancers trip every day," said Ms. Tucker, patting my shoulder. "Then they brush it off, and the show goes on."

I hurried backstage, my face burning, and pulled my street shoes back on. I was never going to go back on that stage. The kids' laughter was still echoing in my ears.

As Pari, Sophie, and I walked out of school to the pickup

area near the big oak tree, I said, "You two should just do this without me."

"What?" Sophie stopped in her tracks and stared at me as if I'd suddenly grown a beard. "Are you kidding? Because of that silly fall?"

"Kavi, remember that time I fell in dance class last month?" said Pari. "Rina Auntie always says, we get back on our feet and carry on."

That was the same thing Ms. Tucker had said. But it didn't matter.

"You're not even hurt," said Sophie. "What's the big deal?"

"Did you hear all the kids laughing at me?" I said.

"Yes," said Sophie. "They laughed at Ali too, when he messed up his juggling act, but he's not dropping out."

"I just can't do it," I repeated. The pressure over school, and now this—it was All. Too. Much.

Pari frowned with concern. "Kavi, we've worked so hard, and you wanted to do this so badly," she said. "I don't get it. What's going on?"

I didn't know how to explain it to them. Fortunately, their rides arrived, so I didn't have to.

After they left, I must have looked upset, because Jake walked up to me and asked, "Are you okay?"

I flushed with embarrassment. "Sorry about hitting you at rehearsal with that yardstick," I mumbled.

"No worries," he shrugged. "It didn't hurt at all."

Suddenly, the words I couldn't find before came tumbling

out. "I've been messing up everything. My schoolwork, and now the dance," I admitted.

"It's not that big a deal, Kavi," Jake said, as if he could see the worry on my face. "Really, it's okay."

I wanted to believe him. But it felt impossible. Right now, nothing was okay. And it was all my fault.

At home, I got out of Dadima's car and went up to my room.

"I don't feel well," I said to Dadima when she came up a few minutes later to check on me.

She touched my forehead. "You don't have a fever. You're just tired from your long day. Rest a bit, and you'll feel better," she said as she left the room.

Scamper came in, wagging his tail and happy to see me as always.

"Scamp," I said, "I quit the revue."

Scamper tilted his head, questioning me with his soft eyes. Even my loyal dog didn't understand why I'd quit. Exhausted, I fell on the bed.

My phone pinged. It was Sophie.

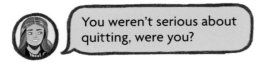

You weren't serious about quitting, were you?

I didn't reply. I *was* serious.

Fifteen minutes later, another message from Sophie:

> We've worked so hard. Accidents happen. It was the silly yardstick. C'mon girl, shake it off.

Shake it off? Easy for her to say. She didn't know about all the other ways in which I'd messed up. She had no idea.

I didn't reply.

A half hour later, Pari texted:

> Hey, I'm here for you. I know you're not a quitter.

I read her message with teary eyes, wishing I could explain how I felt. I couldn't bear the thought of messing up onstage in front of everyone—especially in front of my family. I was already a disappointment to them, and this would just make it worse. I texted back:

> You and Sophie can just dance without me.

My phone pinged immediately.

> What????? No way. This whole thing was YOUR idea. And we've put in many many hours TOGETHER!

And fifteen minutes later:

> If you quit, I'm not dancing. And YOU need to tell Ms. Tucker.

Pari was mad. Sophie didn't get it. There was nothing I could say to make them understand.

I pulled the covers over my head, hugged my pillow, and felt hot tears begin to trickle out.

Suddenly I thought of *Wicked*, when Glinda and Elphaba stopped being friends. I couldn't imagine not being friends with Sophie and Pari. Would they stop being friends with me?

I was awakened by Dad's hand on my shoulder. "Kavi," he said, "Dadima said you aren't feeling well. What's wrong?"

The words escaped my mouth before I could think. "I'm a loser," I told him. "I've screwed up everything."

"Oh beta," he said, sitting down beside me. "You're not a loser, but I want to hear why you think that."

Scamper leaped onto his lap so Dad could rub his chin.

"I wish I was a dog," I said. "I wish I was Scamp."

"Well, who doesn't wish that," said Dad with a smile. "Scamper's life is the best."

"Dad, did you ever mess everything up when you were my age?" I asked.

"Oh Kavi," he said, "once my father was so mad at me, I thought that he'd send me to live with Raj Uncle."

I worried that my parents would be disappointed and unhappy with me, but I never thought they'd pack me off to live with an aunt or uncle. "Why?" I asked.

"I fell far behind in school, and I felt so overwhelmed that I cut school for three days," said Dad. "When my father found out, he was fit to be tied. Raj Uncle had a disciplined military background, and my father thought I might learn a thing or two."

I gaped at Dad in amazement. "Did he really send you to live with your strict uncle?"

"No," said Dad with a smile. "Your dadima didn't let him."

"Arun, Kavi," Mom called from downstairs. "Dinner in five."

"Mom and Dadima have made mouthwatering kebabs," he said. "They'll be hurt if you don't eat."

My stomach rumbled. I hadn't had a snack after school. I got up and splashed some water on my face, then quietly joined everyone at the table.

At dinner, Rishi told a story about their classroom frog. "Why is Mr. Toad a liar?" asked Rishi. When none of us answered, he delivered the punch line: "Because he's an am-*fib*-ian." Fortunately everyone else laughed, so Rishi didn't notice that I hadn't, even though I thought the joke was cute.

Midway through the meal, Mom turned to me and asked, "How was your day, Kavi?"

No more fibbing for me. I swallowed my bite and announced, "I'm going to drop out of the revue."

"What?" Dad said.

Mom said, "Hello? I don't understand."

Even Rishi looked stunned.

Way to go, Kavi, I said to myself. *Way to ruin a nice family dinner.*

Dadima said, "Kavi, I'm so surprised. You love dancing! At *Wicked*, you looked ready to go up on that stage and join in!"

Mom and Dad exchanged a look. "Can you tell us why?" asked Dad.

I swallowed and shook my head. I just couldn't explain, and I didn't want them to feel worse than they already felt. Or maybe *I* didn't want to feel worse by talking about it.

Then, very calmly, measuring each word, Mom said, "It's your decision to make. We're here if you want to talk about it." When Mom was that calm, I knew she was truly concerned.

The silence was pierced by Rishi's shrill voice. "So you're quitting? Just like that? *Kavi has quitteritis*," he sang.

"Rishi," Dad said, "go to your room."

Rishi left, still singing *"quitteritis!"* under his breath.

"Kavi," Dad began.

But I didn't want to hear or say anything more. What was there to say? I fled to my room, again.

Namaste

Chapter 7

Saturday morning, I woke up early and tiptoed down-stairs. As I ate my buttered toast and jam, Dad walked into the kitchen.

"Kavi, do you want to come to my yoga class with me?" he asked.

Dad has attended yoga on Saturday mornings for as long as I can remember. Occasionally, when Dadima was here to watch us, Mom went with him. He'd never asked *me* along before.

"Sure, I guess so," I said. It was better than sitting in my room doing homework. And now that my friends were mad at me, what else was I going to do?

As we drove to the yoga studio, Dad said, "My father was my first yoga teacher. We'd practice the poses in our basement in the Edison house, where Dadima still lives. We didn't have yoga mats or yoga pants. We just spread out a blanket, and I wore my loose pajama pants."

"How did your father learn yoga?" I asked.

"Yoga began in India centuries ago," said Dad. "He learned in school as a kid growing up in India. So did Dadima."

"I didn't know that," I said. "It's for exercise, right?"

"Yoga does help tone the body, but it also helps calm the mind," said Dad.

"Do you think I'll be able to do it?" I asked, suddenly feeling anxious. "I don't want to embarrass myself in class."

"You won't," said Dad as he parked the car. "Yoga is a practice, not a performance. You do it at your own pace. There are no mirrors, and nobody will be watching you except the instructor."

The yoga studio was in a plain building in a strip mall. Inside, the teacher greeted us with "Namaste," which is a traditional Indian greeting of respect. Dad said lots of people who practice yoga use it, even if they're not Indian.

"Namaste," Dad replied. "Kavi, this is Seemaji, my yoga instructor," Dad introduced me. "This is my daughter, Kavi." As other students trickled in, Dad and I unfurled our mats in the back row. I didn't want to be up front my first time.

Seemaji turned on soothing music and spoke in her calm voice. "I see some new faces here. Welcome! Yoga is for you, so only do what feels comfortable for your body. Let's begin in a seated position like lotus pose, and take deep cleansing breaths. Inhale through your nose," said Seemaji, and I did. "Exhale through your mouth, and let go of all the stress."

With each breath, I found myself relaxing a little more. We warmed up on all fours, arching like a cat and swaying our backs like a cow. Then we did poses, which Seemaji called *asanas*. Some of them reminded me of movements that I had learned in dance class. Others were tricky, making me stretch and balance at the same time. Holding those positions required total focus, and I couldn't think about anything else except my body and my breathing. Following the teacher's lead, I was a mountain, a tree, a warrior, a frog, and of course a downward-facing dog—my favorite pose, because it made me think of Scamper. Also, I liked the way my head hanging down let me see the world from a new angle.

By the end of the hour, I had learned a whole new way of breathing, and I felt amazingly relaxed.

After class, we decided to stop by the samosa shop on our way home. I linked arms with Dad as we walked back out to the car. "Can I come back next Saturday?"

"I was hoping you'd want to," he said with a grin.

"Can we also get samosas after class next week?" I asked, taking a bite. The flaky pastry was buttery and delicious.

"That's a deal," said Dad, and he took a bite, too.

As we drove home, I said, "Dad, when I forget things, Dadima says I remind her of you when you were my age. What does she mean?"

For a moment Dad seemed to be lost in the past. Then he said, "I was often forgetful, just like you. Focusing and organizing my schoolwork wasn't easy." He smiled. "My room was not as messy as yours, but that was because I shared the room with my sister, and she organized it." Dad continued. "Hasan Uncle was in my class, and he'd kick my

chair when I wasn't attentive. I used to get annoyed with him for doing that, but he kept me on task."

Hasan Uncle and Dad were still best friends. Hasan Uncle wasn't Dad's brother, but we called him uncle out of respect.

Dad explained, "Back in those days, my teachers and parents just thought I was lazy and that I could do better if I tried harder. They thought I was just being a boy. I liked to crack jokes and was a bit of a class clown," Dad went on. "The truth was, I needed to move, to fidget. Eventually, I realized that doodling helped me focus. Some of my teachers thought I was goofing off when I was doodling—but actually, it was helping me pay attention. I also got really good at drawing, which helped me become an architect."

Again, I thought about *Wicked* and its message that talents could be used for good or bad—and that sometimes it's hard to tell the difference.

"Dad, there's a boy in my class, Jake, who sounds sort of like you were as a kid," I said. "He fidgets and moves around all the time. When I told him it was distracting, he told me it's just how his brain works." I paused, then added, "Maybe his brain is like yours. Maybe mine is, too."

Dad looked thoughtful. "That could be. Everyone's brain is a little different. That's what makes each of us unique, and why we all have different interests and abilities."

"And different problems," I added.

He smiled. "Yes, sometimes. But remember, that's

what makes you *you*. The trick is to find a way to channel your special qualities into the things you love, so that they become part of your talents, instead of a problem to solve. Just like my doodling helped me become a good architect."

Was Dad right? Could my unique brain help make me better at school? Or at being a performer?

I thought of the cloud dances that Sophie, Pari, and I had created. They had definitely helped me ace the science test. But after my fall at that last rehearsal, I didn't see how *anything* could help me get back up onstage.

That night as I got ready for bed, the thought of the revue came rushing back. I still needed to let Ms. Tucker know I wasn't going to dance. What would she think of me dropping out? I dreaded the thought of telling her.

Since Pari had already refused, I texted Sophie: *Will you go with me tomorrow to tell Ms. Tucker about my dropping out of the revue?* I waited, but she didn't text back.

Well, it's late, I told myself. *Maybe she'll reply tomorrow.*

On Sunday morning, there was still no word from Sophie. She had never ignored me like this before. Apparently I was on my own with telling Ms. Tucker that I was dropping out of the revue. I would have to tell Rina Auntie at dance class on Tuesday, too. *Ugh.*

In the kitchen, Mom was packing a blanket, towels, and thermoses of coffee and hot chocolate in a basket. "We're going to Asbury Park for the day," she announced, as Rishi danced around the kitchen with excitement.

I looked outside. It was early November, but the weather was still mild and the sun was shining.

"This family has had some big changes recently. I think we need a break, a day to just chill and hear the roar of the ocean," Mom said, as we all went to the garage and climbed into the car.

"Couldn't agree with you more," said Dad.

"I love going to Asbury Park after the season," said Mom. "It's so much nicer."

She was right. The boardwalk wasn't crowded. Some of the souvenir shops were still open on the weekend. The beach was mostly deserted, except for some walkers and a few families. Rishi and I took off our shoes. The water was too cold for wading, but it was still fun to feel the sand between my toes. The wind lifting my hair and stinging my face and the roar and smell of the ocean felt delicious. It was very different from going to the beach in the summer, but I decided I liked it just as much.

Rishi asked me to bury his legs in the sand, so I did. The crisp wind and the exercise made me hungry. As Rishi emerged from the sand and brushed himself off, his stomach rumbled. "Food!" he moaned.

We went to our favorite pizza place. When our drinks arrived, Mom cleared her throat and tapped her spoon on her glass. "I want to thank you all for helping me return to work," she said. "It's going well, and I love my new job. To be honest, parts of the job are hard, and I'm playing catch-up, but I'm really enjoying being back in a lab."

"You mean you're not going to quit your job?" I blurted out. "Because of me?"

Mom's eyes were huge. "Whatever made you think that, Kavi?"

Oops. I gave myself away. Now I needed to fess up.

"I overheard you and Dad talking," I mumbled. "After the parent-teacher conferences."

"Oh, Kavi," said Mom, shaking her head. "I'm sorry you heard that. Listening to grown-ups' conversations is not a good idea."

I knew she was right. "Sorry," I said.

She reached over and took my hand in forgiveness, saying, "I know the adjustment has been challenging for us all. But we Sharmas are strong and don't give up easily. Thank you for making it possible for me to do what I love."

Rishi clapped, and Dad reached across the table and held Mom's other hand. I flushed with embarrassment and pride. The pizza arrived just then, and the gooey richness of the cheese silenced us all as we dug in.

After our late lunch, as we were heading back to the car, I noticed a mural of a girl on the side of a building. She

wore a red skirt, and a dark blue sky stretched behind her, with stars and flowers scattered across it. I made everyone wait while I took pictures of it.

The girl's outfit reminded me of an outfit that Pari had worn for Diwali last year. At the thought of Pari, my throat tightened. Was she still angry with me?

I picked the best photo I'd taken of the mural and sent it to Pari, hoping it would remind her of her outfit. I checked my phone an hour later, and every hour after that, until I went to bed, but there was no reply.

Brains, Heart, Courage
Chapter 8

The next morning, with crossed fingers, I checked my phone one last time before school. Pari had replied!

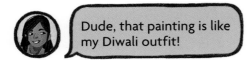

Dude, that painting is like my Diwali outfit!

I exhaled with relief and whooped with joy. The old me would have danced around the room until Mom stepped in and reminded me to get ready for school. But I resisted the urge. I couldn't miss the bus, so I put my phone away and continued to dress.

Mom's words from yesterday echoed in my head. *Thank you for making it possible for me to do what I love.*

I loved to dance—and my friends were the ones who had made it possible for me to dance in the revue. Even shy Pari, who hadn't really wanted to, had agreed to do it when I begged her. Pari wasn't doing it for herself, I realized—she was doing it for me. It was a gift she was giving me, to make me happy.

And I had thrown her gift to me back in her face by quitting.

We Sharmas are strong and don't give up easily. Mom hadn't let a setback like her daughter's school struggles stop her from doing what she loved. Why should I let a silly little thing like falling onstage stop me?

On the bus, Pari sat down beside me without saying a word and showed me a picture on her phone. I gasped. It was Pari and her sister, wearing matching outfits—a long red skirt with a gold pattern and a sparkly sequined top— the very same outfit that looked like the girl in the mural.

The bus screeched to a halt in front of the school with its usual wheezing and lurch. We got off and entered the building. As we walked down the corridor, I imagined Pari and me wearing those outfits, dancing in the revue, and my family sitting in the front row beaming with pride. I took a breath and paused. I realized that I didn't need to see Ms. Tucker to tell her that I was dropping out of the revue.

Because I wasn't.

I pivoted, spinning on my heels, and linked arms with Pari, who hadn't said a word all this time. "Pari," I announced, "I'm not dropping out of the revue."

"Really?" said Pari, her face lighting up.

"Rishi said I have quitteritis," I told her.

Pari groaned. "Rishi is hilarious, and he's brutally hon- est." She gave me a hug. "I can't wait to practice with you in dance class. We're doing this, girl!"

The bell rang. As we walked to homeroom, I reminded

myself that I was a Sharma. That meant I was strong, and I didn't give up easily.

On Tuesday after school, we went to Pari's house so her mom could drive us to dance class.

As we walked into Pari's bedroom and set down our backpacks, she said, "Guess what—Priya's old Diwali outfit matched mine! Let's see if it fits you. Maybe we could wear them Maybe we could wear them in the revue!"

"Ooh, yes!" I agreed. I slipped on the outfit and looked at myself in the mirror. The blouse hung on my frame, the skirt was too long—I could trip over the hem. Priya was a junior in high school and quite a bit bigger than me. Disappointed, I turned around so Pari could assess.

"Not bad at all!" she said.

"Really?" I said lifting the too-long skirt.

"Amma," Pari called. "Amma, we have a sewing project for you!" Pari calls her mother *Amma,* which means "mother" in most South Indian languages.

Mrs. Nath came bustling in. When she saw the outfit on me, she said, "Kavi, ask your mother if you can come back here after dance class. You can do homework with Pari and eat dinner with us. I'll start altering the outfit while you girls are at class." She got out a fabric chalk and lots of pins, and pinned the skirt and top to fit me.

I quickly texted Mom, who sent a thumbs-up. "She says

I can stay! Thank you so much," I told Pari's mother.

"Good. I hope you like *dosas*," said Mrs. Nath with a wink. Clearly she remembered that I loved the crispy lentil crepe with all the savory dipping sauces. I'd eaten them at Pari's house before. "Now let's get you dancers to your class."

Later that evening, before Pari's father drove me home, Mrs. Nath had me try on the outfit again. It was perfect, as if it had been created for me. And, in a way, it was.

Although I had managed to do better on the last few science quizzes, thanks to doing my homework, I still needed to do really well on the big end-of-unit test. Not only to bring up my grade, but also to prove to my parents—and myself—that I could succeed in the hard classes I was taking. So after school, I studied at the kitchen table with Dadima, and when Mom came home, I asked her to quiz me on the scientific method.

"Didi has scholaritis," said Rishi.

"Thanks for the accurate diagnosis, Dr. Sharma!" I replied.

Sophie and Pari were studying for the test too, so we did a group chat. We chanted our mnemonic for remembering the scientific method: "Ouch, Hey Ed, That's Loud," which stood for Observation, Hypothesis, Experiments, Theory, and Law. I loved our nerdy ways.

The night before the test, I went to bed early to be well rested. (It's not just beauty sleep; it's for your brain, too!)

The test wasn't easy, but I was pretty sure I knew most of the answers or at least knew how to figure them out. For once, the test actually felt like a reward for studying instead of a punishment for messing up.

After it was over, I was dying to know how I had done. It was hard waiting to find out!

After school the next day, while Rishi was at soccer practice, Dadima took Pari, Sophie, and me shopping in Edison, which has blocks of Indian groceries, restaurants, and stores that sell saris, tablecloths, bedspreads, paper star lanterns, incense, jewelry, and other goods from India. We were shopping for parasols for our dance. One store had parasols hanging upside down from the ceiling to make it easier to see the designs. They were all so dazzling, it was difficult to choose!

"Look at that one over there," said Sophie. "It has little elephants on it, just like your Hattie."

"Ooh, yes!" I said. "I love elephants."

"Me too!" said Pari.

"We'll take three of those," Dadima told the shopkeeper, and ta-da, our costumes were complete.

On Thursday, Mr. Proton handed us our graded tests.
When I saw the paper with the big red A and a smiley face,
I let out a whoop of joy. I showed it to my friends, who had
also gotten A's, and we group-hugged.

At lunch, I texted a photo of the test to my parents, who
texted back: 😃 👏

Now there was no shred of doubt that I could be in the
revue. Which was in just two days—*eeek!*

Friday night after dinner, Sophie and Pari came over so
that Mom could paint traditional Indian henna designs on
our hands. We had poses during the dance when we would
open our hands toward the audience so that they could see
the beautiful designs. Even though Sophie isn't Indian, Mom
was painting her hands, too, because we are a trio and didn't
want to leave her out of the fun. Henna is for everyone.

Sophie said she felt honored to be included.

Mom used a special cone with a fine tip. The cone is like a piping bag for decorating cakes, except it contains a red-brown paste made from henna leaves rather than icing. The paste makes a reddish-brown stain on the skin that lasts for days. Eucalyptus oil gives it a spicy aroma that I like, but Pari wrinkled her nose at the smell as Mom carefully piped a pattern of flowers and leaves on her hand. Next it was Sophie's turn, and then mine. Rishi got an armband of flames. After an hour, we scraped off the sticky henna paste, leaving a beautiful deep, rich, red pattern on our hands.

We were ready for the revue.

"Hurry up, Saturday," I said to Hattie as I turned off the lights that night. I was nervous, yet excited. I couldn't wait!

Five-Six-Seven-Eight!
Chapter 9

On Saturday after a very early dinner, Pari and her mom drove over with our beautiful dance outfits. Our moms helped us with our stage makeup. A bit of lipstick, a touch of shimmery gold eye shadow, and some color on our cheeks—that was the usual for a Bollywood dance performance.

Rishi told me, "You look like a superstar." For once, he didn't call it a disease!

"Why, thank you, Rishi," I replied. "I'd be happy to give you an autograph."

Sophie arrived dressed in her dance outfit, which coordinated with ours, with a sparkly blue top. Dadima brought out her assortment of stick-on bindis and scattered them on my bed. A *bindi* is a dot of color worn on the forehead or between the eyebrows. Dadima had quite a collection. Some were round, some were oval or tear-shaped. Some had little jewels on them.

"I know it's traditional to wear these," said Sophie, "but what do they mean?"

"The bindi is worn by women all over India and South Asia," Dadima explained. "It represents the seat of wisdom, sometimes known as the third eye."

"They're all so pretty. It's hard to choose," said Pari. "My aunts in India wear one every day, as a sign that they're married."

"Do they wear wedding rings too?" asked Sophie curiously.

Pari nodded. "The bindi is a traditional symbol of marriage, while the wedding ring is more modern. Only some of my aunts wear rings, but they all wear bindis."

Pari and I chose matching round red bindis—the simple, basic shape. We placed them onto our foreheads, between the brows, and spun around in our *lehengas*. The red-and-gold skirts flared out, shimmering.

"Dadima," I said, "we'll show everyone the beauty of our culture."

"And I'll be the proud grandma in the audience," said Dadima. "Now I better go get ready, too!"

Half an hour later, Sophie and Pari left with their parents, and Dad, Mom, Rishi, Dadima, and I got into Dad's car.

"Ready to rock and roll?" Dad asked.

"Everyone have everything?" Mom chimed in.

I looked through my bag. Hairbrush, bobby pins, and water bottle—check, check, and check.

Then it struck me. "Stop! Dad! Stop the car!"

The car screeched to a halt.

"My parasol," I gasped. "I forgot my parasol!"

Dad reversed into the driveway. I grabbed the house keys from Mom and dashed back into the house. The elephant parasol was in my room, waiting for me. I grabbed it and hurried out.

"Got it!" I called, holding up the folded parasol like a trophy. I climbed back into the car, and we were off.

In the hallway outside the auditorium, I got a group hug from my family as we parted ways.

"Break a leg!" Rishi called after me as I headed for the dressing room.

Backstage was a beehive of activity, with everyone buzzing around. Pari, Sophie, and I took selfies in the makeup mirror, and then went over our dance steps in

a corner of the room. Jake was pacing in another corner, reading from flash cards and going over his jokes. A girl was tuning her violin, and I could hear a clarinet playing scales and tap shoes clacking on the concrete floor. A ballet dancer silently practiced her pirouettes.

In the midst of all the chaos, Ali was juggling intently. He caught the colored balls one by one, and I applauded and gave him a thumbs-up. He waved back and gave me a thumbs-up, too. In the silent language of theater people, I knew that we were telling each other, *Forget about past mistakes. You got this!*

We could hear the audience coming in, chairs squeaking and scratching as people took their seats. Then the lights dimmed, the audience hushed, and the performers backstage fell silent. Ms. Tucker stepped onstage to welcome everyone.

I stood in the wings, peeking out at the audience. My family was in the front row. Dadima was glamorous in her shimmering silk sari and jeweled bindi. Her face beamed with pride as the revue began.

After the elegant ballet dancers, Jake's comedy act brought down the house. Then Ali walked to center stage juggling four balls with a swagger in his step, his eyes firmly on the balls flying above his hands as jaunty music played. I clutched Pari's hand. Both of us wanted Ali to succeed. As he added a fifth ball, there was a moment when I thought he was going to drop it, and I almost gasped aloud. But he leaned out and grabbed the ball in an impressive save and kept the juggling act going smoothly. The audience applauded. In the front row, Rishi's eyes were huge. For his grand finale, Ali brought out a skateboard and juggled while skating in a circle. The audience went crazy, clapping in rhythm to the music.

Then it was our turn. The butterflies in my stomach fluttered their wings as Sophie nudged Pari and me forward. I knew Pari was even more nervous than I was as we stepped out into the spotlight. Together, Pari and I read a paragraph explaining the meaning of our song. It celebrated victory after a long and difficult battle and wished everyone peace, prosperity, and happiness.

Then the music came on, the drums loud and hypnotic.

"A five-six-seven-eight," Pari counted under her breath, and we ran to the front of the stage, twirling our open parasols.

An "*Ohhh!*" rose from the audience.

Our performance started out with traditional Indian music and dancing—then, suddenly, the music became jazzier. We closed the parasols and set them aside as Sophie joined us, and then the three of us launched into our Bollywood routine.

We put everything we had into each step; our expressions and movements conveyed everything from anguish to joy. Soon, the audience was clapping along. The difficult step that had tripped me up before was a mere second

away. I took a deep breath and grabbed my parasol. *Spin,
slide, open the parasol, spin it, and dance around each other.* As
the end approached, we lifted our parasols high and spun,
our skirts twirling. The audience clapped and cheered as
Sophie, Pari, and I took a bow and raced off the stage.

After the revue was over, the lobby was loud with joy as
families greeted their performers. I saw Alaina, the amazing singer in the second act, surrounded by admiring fans.
Ali hugged me and said, "Bravo, Kavi!"

I hugged him back, saying, "Bravo to you, too. You
totally nailed it!" as Rishi came up and asked Ali for his
autograph.

Jake said, "Whoa, Kavi! Who knew you were a dancer?"

I grinned and replied, "Thanks! I already knew you
were a comedian—but now the whole world knows!"

Rina Auntie rushed toward us and handed each of us
a bouquet of flowers. "Bravo! *Badhai ho!* Congratulations!
You girls were beautiful up there. You should all take my
Bollywood class next year!"

As I looked around at my family and friends, I was
so thankful that I hadn't quit. To think that I would have
missed all this! The thrill of success after all my doubts
and hard work was exhilarating. What a feeling! I could
get used to it.

A New Plan
Chapter 10

One evening after Mom and I had watched our favorite singing talent show while eating ice cream, she said, "Kavi, we need to talk."

I nodded and ate a big spoonful of rocky road with a gulp. *Uh-oh.* "We do?" I asked.

I was afraid of where this conversation was going, but I was also curious to find out what was going on. As Mr. Proton likes to say, "Knowledge empowers us."

"I know that you're twelve and want to be independent, but age is sometimes irrelevant," she said with a smile. "We all need help in life. And right now, you need help with keeping your room and backpack organized."

I nodded. Mom was right. "And I need to ask for help with schoolwork when I need it, and not wait until I fall behind," I admitted.

Mom and I put our heads together. Soon we had a plan:

1. On weekends and Wednesdays, Mom or Dad will check my backpack and room. And I'll ask Dadima for help when she comes over after school.

2. Wednesday nights will be Sharma family tutorial night, for both Rishi and me to go over what we're learning in school with Mom and Dad.
3. Continue to go to yoga with Dad and use the breathing techniques when I feel overwhelmed.

Then Mom and I polished off the last of the ice cream. The road hadn't been as rocky as I feared.

That night, I wrote in my journal:

It's official. I may not be the most organized person, but I'm the most determined. With team Sharma on my side, nothing can stop me.

At school the following week, I met with my counselor, Ms. González. I was nervous about how it would go, but when she started the meeting by offering me a piece of candy from her famous bowl of chocolate kisses, I thought, *Maybe this won't be so bad.*

Ms. González talked about her experience working with lots of different students. "We each have talents and strengths and weaknesses, the same way we each have different skin colors, heights, and athletic abilities. And each of our brains functions differently, too," she said. "We can arrange for you to have extra time with a teacher, or a private room for taking a test. There are lots of options."

I nodded. I had questions, but I was tongue-tied.

"You can come and talk to me whenever you want," she assured me. "The school is here to support you."

The next day, Pari, Sophie, and I set down our trays at our usual table in the noisy cafeteria. I wanted to tell my friends that I might need extra help in school, but I suddenly felt nervous. I stuffed the rest of my chutney and cheese sandwich in my mouth to buy some more time. Finally, I swallowed, took a deep yoga breath, and told them what my counselor had said.

"Is that why your seat was switched in English class?" Pari asked.

I nodded again. "Since you sit behind me now, could you nudge me when it looks like I'm distracted?"

"You got it," said Pari with a grin. "Note to self: Poke Kavi when needed."

I laughed. Pari and Sophie were my Hasan Uncle. They also promised to keep up our group study sessions.

"We'll keep making up dances for new science concepts, just like we did with the clouds," said Sophie.

"Good," I said. "Somehow it helps me learn better."

"Hey, maybe Mr. Proton could post our science dances on his class website," Pari suggested. "They might help other kids learn the concepts, too."

I grinned with relief. My friends were the best.

After the revue was over, I stopped my dance lessons for a while, as my parents and I had agreed. But every Saturday morning, I went to yoga class with Dad. Sometimes Mom dropped Rishi off at a friend's house, and she came to yoga with us.

One Saturday morning in December near the end of yoga class, I was in a twisty pose called Half Lord of the Fishes. My left foot was placed flat on the floor outside my right thigh, with my right leg bent at the knee and my body twisted to the left. I looked like a pretzel, and felt like one, too.

"Look, I'm stuck!" I joked to my parents.

"Sometimes that happens," Dad teased, as Mom reached over and helped me uncurl out of my asana. We were all laughing.

After class, we had our post-yoga ritual, stopping for samosas. I loved our Saturday mornings.

Soon it was winter break. Although I had managed to keep up in my classes with the help of my family and friends, I was exhausted, and grateful to have a break from school.

Dadima came over to stay with Rishi and me while our parents were at work. Rishi and I love cookies, so most days we baked. We made so many cookies that we started delivering them to friends and neighbors.

Once, after we'd taken a batch of cookies and holiday wishes to the family next door, Dadima told us, "Yesterday my neighbor called to thank me and said, 'These cookies are dynamite. I wish I could buy some.'"

"Dadima, she's not the only one who wants to buy them," I replied. "Maybe you should start a business."

"You should," Rishi chimed in. "I would buy them, too."

"You don't need to buy them, Rishi," Dadima said. "But don't you think I'm too old to start a business?"

"Nooo!" Rishi and I said in unison. "Of course you're not."

"What would you call your business?" I asked her.

"The Cookie Jar," she said right away. And that's how I knew she'd been giving the idea serious thought.

"Ooh, I love that name," I said. "We'll help you make the Cookie Jar a big success."

Rishi nodded. "We'll be your official cookie tasters," he said.

"It's a deal," said Dadima. And we shook on it.

Another thing I did over winter break was practice my singing. After hearing how well Alaina Peterson sang in the revue, I felt I should learn and practice more. Mom helped me find some voice lessons online, and I began practicing every day.

Sometimes I'd go to the staircase and start with vocal warm-up exercises. Standing on the bottom step, I sang my favorite phrase, going up the scale: "Mommy made me mash

my m&m's!" Then I stepped up one stair, switched to a higher key, and sang it again. I kept going until I reached my favorite acoustic spot on the landing. Then I was ready to belt out a song.

One evening, after my parents were home from work and making dinner, I stood on the staircase and sang, "Mommy made me mash my m&m's!"

Everyone turned and looked at me.

"Did she now?" said Mom, grinning. Soon, Mom and Dad and Rishi and Dadima, who was staying for dinner that night, were singing the scales with me, while I swung my hands like a conductor. It was the Sharma Family Choir.

At the dinner table, as we dunked our grilled cheese sandwiches in tomato soup, Dadima said, "Kavi, you sing so well. Next time your school does a show, maybe you can sing in it."

I beamed with pride, and after dinner I practiced some more.

Dadima's praise started me thinking. My middle school always put on a big musical in the spring. Last year I hadn't auditioned for it, but now I thought, *Why not?* After all, with the support of my family, friends, and school, I had been able to do the revue and still keep my grades up. And now, with all my singing practice, maybe I could even get a starring role!

Yes, I decided—I would definitely try out for the spring

musical. Now the big question was, which musical would we be doing? And which role could I play? Suddenly, I couldn't wait to get back to school and find out.

The last night of winter break, I looked out at the bare trees. The rain on their branches had frozen, and they glistened like diamonds in the streetlights. I felt excited and a little giddy. A brand-new semester was about to start. Would it bring the success and stardom I dreamed of?

Cookies and Curls

Chapter 11

The next morning, as I waited for the school bus, I remembered the horrible day last fall when I had missed the bus, and all my troubles started. I promised myself that that wouldn't happen again this year!

On the bus, I gave Sophie and Pari little boxes of cookies and told them about how Dadima was thinking of starting a cookie business.

"Your grandmother's cookies are delicious!" said Pari, sampling one. "She should totally do it."

"Yum," agreed Sophie, with her mouth full. "Let me know if she needs someone to taste-test her recipes!"

When we got to school, the first thing I spied in the hallway was a new poster:

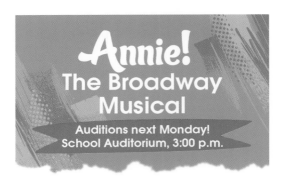

Annie!
The Broadway
Musical
Auditions next Monday!
School Auditorium, 3:00 p.m.

My heart began to beat with excitement. I knew the story was about an orphan girl during the Great Depression—and there she was on the poster, with her curly hair, red dress, and confident grin, her hands plonked on her waist as if she was ready to take on the world with her yellow dog, Sandy.

I'd seen the movie a few years ago with my family. I loved the way Annie transformed from the poor girl living in the orphanage at the beginning of the show to the end, when she's adopted by the rich Mr. Warbucks. I understood Annie's optimism and her belief in a better tomorrow. Annie was so determined and brave when faced with obstacles. She was tough and didn't give up. Like me!

In that moment, I knew that I wanted to be Annie in the show. I could already see myself belting out "Tomorrow."

Pari squeezed my arm. "You're trying out, right?" she asked, and I nodded. "I know I didn't want to be in the revue at first, but I'm glad I did it. It was so much fun. I think I'll audition for the musical, too! Maybe I could play an orphan." Then she turned to Sophie and said, "Sophie, you should audition with us!"

"Oh, I can't sing," said Sophie. "I want to be on the stage crew. I love to paint, so I could help make scenery. But you two should totally go for it!"

Cookies and Curls

On Friday night, Pari and Sophie came for a sleepover, and we watched *Annie* together, with bowls of popcorn. Dadima came over to deliver some cranberry-pecan shortbread cookies. She said she was trying to get them just right. We tasted them thoroughly and judged them to be perfect.

"How's the Cookie Jar coming along?" I asked her.

Dadima sighed. "I have no idea how to get customers and market my cookies," she admitted. "I'm not good with social media. I've never made videos like you kids do all the time. I wouldn't know how to begin."

"I'll make a commercial for you," I offered.

"My sister Priya's good at making videos," said Pari. "She could shoot it for you, and then she could post the video on her social media accounts."

"That would be wonderful," said Dadima. "I accept your offer, and I'll pay you all in cookies!"

"Dadima, you've got a deal," I told her.

We went back to the movie. We watched the orphans' song about the "hard-knock life" twice, singing and dancing along for practice. Then we sang "Tomorrow." It was so much fun! Now I wanted to be Annie even more.

"I need to look more like Annie," I told Pari and Sophie after the movie. "My hair is nothing like hers. Hers is super curly all over."

They agreed it might help my audition if I looked more like Annie. We decided to practice with Mom's curling iron.

Sophie said she had curled her cousin's hair once, so she combed my hair into sections and started. Twirl, twirl, twirl, hold . . . release.

"Hmm, it's not working," said Sophie. "Maybe we need a better curling iron."

"We need help from Priya," said Pari. "She does all kinds of stuff with her hair. I'll tell her to come over tomorrow."

On Saturday it snowed. It was the fluffy, pretty kind, just an inch or two. The yard looked like a winter fairyland—perfect for shooting a cookie commercial.

Priya came over after breakfast, and we all got dressed

for the shoot. My backup singers, Pari, Sophie, and Rishi, wore blue jackets, red scarves, and white earmuffs. Since I was the lead singer, I wore my furry jacket and matching earmuffs. Priya, the director, had a clipboard and her phone. Scamper could barely believe that we were all out in the snow with him and romped about with excitement.

Priya said, "Places, everyone. Recording in five ... four ... three ... two ... one!"

I stood in front, with Rishi, Sophie, and Pari behind me. We all held cookies. I smiled brightly at the camera and launched into my song:

> *I love these cookies,*
> *these crispy, chewy cookies.*
> *You'll love these cookies,*
> *these sweet, crunchy cookies.*
> *They're simply irresistible—*
> *and oh so yummy!*

And the backup singers crooned, "*Yummy, yummy cookies! Mmmm!*"

We each took a bite of our cookies, and then Scamper raced to me, jumped up, grabbed my cookie, and gulped it down.

"Cut!" said Priya.

The take was perfect. Priya said she would add pricing information and ordering instructions at the end of the commercial before she posted it.

"And now, Kavi," she said as we headed back inside, "I

hear you want curls for the audition on Monday."

She had brought her curlers and hair stuff in a duffel bag. We all trooped upstairs to my bedroom.

Priya draped a towel over my shoulders and got to work. I imagined myself with a glorious head of tight, magnificent curls. Even though they wouldn't be red like Annie's, they would be close enough to give the idea, unlike my long, straight hair. And this way, Ms. Tucker would see that I was perfect for the role.

"Kavi, leave the curlers in all night," Priya said. "Tomorrow morning, you can take them out."

Sleeping with curlers is not the easiest thing to do, but I knew it would be worth it. "Tomorrow" played in my dreams as I let the curlers do their magic.

The next morning, as Mom carefully removed the curlers from my head, I closed my eyes, waiting to be amazed by my headful of bouncy, beautiful ringlets.

"Tell me when to look," I said.

I heard a soft gasp. *Oooh*, I thought with anticipation. *Mom must think my hair looks nice and curly, just like Annie's!*

Then I heard Rishi say, "Zoinks!"

My eyes flew open. "Eeek!" I gasped. In the mirror, some of my hair was tightly curled and hung in coiled springs around my head. The other part looked as if I'd been struck by lightning and the electricity had gone out

my hair. Definitely *not* the look I was going for!

Mom began to laugh. "Oh, Kavi," she said, "aren't you glad it's only hair? The curls can be straightened."

"You have to admit it's epic, though," said Rishi, his eyes wide. "Too bad it's not Halloween!"

I had to agree that I looked ridiculous. Despite my disappointment, I couldn't help laughing at how silly I looked. Fortunately, water and shampoo brought my hair back to normal.

Oh well, so my hair wasn't going to impress Ms. Tucker at the audition. I would have to rely on my singing and dancing to earn the role of Annie.

A Hard-Knock Life
Chapter 12

After school on Monday, I pushed open the heavy door and stepped into the auditorium for the audition. Ms. Tucker and Miss Clarke, the choir director, sat in the first row, opposite the stage. I felt nervous and excited as I looked around the room at the four other girls auditioning for the role of Annie. They were all eighth-graders. One of them was Alaina Peterson, the one who sang like an angel in the revue.

Each actor auditioning for the role of Annie had to sing two songs, dance a short routine, and then act out a scene from the play with Ms. Tucker, who read the other character's lines. When it was my turn, my legs felt like jelly as I climbed up the steps to the stage. *You can do this*, I told myself.

My singing practice had paid off. My voice was smooth, and I hit the high notes. Halfway through my second song, I saw Ms. Tucker and Miss Clarke whispering and jotting comments on their clipboards.

I stumbled once while reading the dialogue, but at least I didn't mess up the dance steps. I gave my audition a solid B-plus, relieved that it was over. I had done my best.

"Thank you, Kavi," said Miss Clarke. People said that

Miss Clarke had once sung on Broadway. Maybe, I thought, if I could learn the ropes from her, this would be my first step toward performing on Broadway one day.

When Alaina came onstage and began to sing, I watched, mesmerized. Her voice was so beautiful. She paused at all the right places, holding the notes like the singers on the talent shows Mom and I liked to watch on TV. Alaina danced well, too. And when she acted out the scene with Ms. Tucker, she made me believe that there was a dog with her. I had to admit, it was an A-plus performance.

My confidence wavered. Did I have any chance of being selected to play Annie?

"Thank you, Alaina," said Miss Clarke.

I couldn't imagine anyone wanting to be Annie as much as I did. But I had to face it: I had tough competition.

Two days later, at lunch, a buzz flew around the cafeteria. The cast list was up! I rushed out of the cafeteria with Pari and Sophie.

In the hallway, I saw a group of kids high-fiving Alaina Peterson. With my heart pounding in my ears, I read the list.

Annie: Alaina Peterson

Alaina had gotten the lead role. Although I couldn't pretend, even to myself, that she didn't deserve it, I felt like a deflated balloon falling to the floor.

Suddenly I heard a shriek of happiness, and Pari clutched my arm and shrieked again. "Kavi!" she said. "Look—we're both orphans!" Her face was lit up with joy and excitement.

"I'm on the stage crew!" Sophie exclaimed, hugging us both. "This is going to be so much fun!"

I forced myself to smile despite the huge lump of disappointment stuck in my throat. Pari and I had small roles as unnamed orphans. We would sing and dance and act, but we had no lines.

During class, my eyes blurred with unshed tears. I wasn't going to be Annie. I was just a nameless orphan. After all the hours of practice, my voice would barely be heard, drowned out in the chorus of voices with Pari and the other orphans.

I looked at the rehearsal schedule and sighed. Did I even want to do this? I knew it would be a lot of work. We would have rehearsals after school three days a week. Was it worth it?

When I got home, Rishi asked me, "Did you get a part in the play?"

I nodded. "I'm one of the orphans."

"Just like Scamper was when he showed up at our door," said Rishi.

Scamper had wandered into our backyard several

years ago. He didn't have a microchip, we couldn't find his humans, and within a day he'd found a home in all our hearts. We didn't know we needed a dog until he showed up. Was it possible I needed this part but didn't know it?

It didn't seem very likely. The show certainly didn't need me. There were plenty of other orphans, and the show would be exactly the same whether I was in it or not.

Rishi announced my role as an orphan as soon as Mom and Dad got home. Their faces lit up with pride.

"Our Kavi is in the spring musical!" said Dad.

"How wonderful!" said Mom. "Congratulations!"

"Pari is one of the orphans too," I said, "and she's thrilled about it. But I wanted to play Annie."

"Of course she's thrilled," said Mom. "It will be fun! I always wanted to try out for a play but I never did. Auditioning isn't easy; both of you should be very proud of getting a part on your first try!"

At least my family was taking it well, even if I wasn't.

Then Mom and Dad saw the ambitious rehearsal schedule on the kitchen counter.

"Hmm, that's a big commitment," said Mom.

"You'll have to stay super organized to keep up with your schoolwork and all of this," said Dad.

"I'll use my planner and set reminders on my phone, and I'll ask for help if I need it," I promised.

To myself I thought, *If it gets to be too much, I can always drop out. The show would go on just fine without me.*

After dinner and homework, I went to the keyboard. Maybe I couldn't sing a solo in the show, but no one could stop me from singing one in my living room. I picked out the tune of the orphans' song, "It's the Hard-Knock Life," and softly sang the words, resigned to my fate, like the orphans.

Did I catch Mom and Dad exchanging a smile? They didn't understand that there was nothing to smile about. Joy tastes like pistachio ice cream. Disappointment tastes like day-old tea, bitter and stale.

At our first rehearsal, Ms. Tucker asked all the cast and crew members to make a big circle. "Will this show be fun?" she asked.

"Yes!" we said.

"That didn't sound convincing," she said. "Will this show be the best?"

"YES!!!!!" we roared.

Ms. Tucker had us go around the circle and say our names and roles. At the end, she said, "You may have noticed that I didn't cast anyone to play Sandy, the dog. I thought it would be fun to have a real dog play Sandy. I'm hoping—" Before she had even finished speaking, Alaina's hand shot up.

"Finley!" said Alaina. "That's my dog. Finley would make a perfect Sandy, because she knows me!"

Ms. Tucker said, "Wonderful! She'll need to rehearse with us when we're ready."

Alaina nodded, beaming.

What? Just like that? No audition? I remembered Scamper's flawless performance in our cookie commercial. It was so unfair—even Alaina's *dog* was getting a starring role.

With the casting of Sandy squared away, Ms. Tucker moved on. "Let's work hard. Let's have fun. Let's make this a great show!"

We all clapped. The room was full of happy faces. I pretended to be just as thrilled as my castmates.

The Show Must Go On
Chapter 13

The following Monday when I got home from rehearsal, I was greeted by the smell of chocolate chip cookies and the sound of the stand mixer hard at work. Cookie trays with baked and unbaked cookies covered every surface. Dadima had streaks of flour in her hair. "Hello!" I shouted over the sound of the mixer.

Dadima turned it off and said, "Kavi, since Priya posted your commercial, I've gotten more orders than my small kitchen can handle."

"Hooray!" I said. "Can I help?"

"Yes, you and Rishi can box the cookies," said Dadima, pointing to a pile of folded boxes. Carefully, Rishi and I put a dozen cookies in each box. We saved all the broken bits (that didn't end up in our mouths) for dessert that night.

Rehearsals were on Mondays, Tuesdays, and Thursdays. Ms. Tucker always warmed us up with theater games and exercises to loosen up our bodies and build trust among the actors. She encouraged us to do our homework while we waited to rehearse our scenes. Pari and I studied together at the back of the auditorium. I wore my headphones, so I could focus on my homework.

Miss Clarke led us through voice warm-ups every day and gave us tips on keeping our voices strong. "Kavi, protect your vocal chords—they are your instrument," she said once when she heard me shouting across the room to my friends. I'd never thought of my voice that way before.

The rehearsals flew by. When I wasn't onstage or doing homework, I watched the actors in lead roles practice their dialogue. Jake was playing one of the policemen. He was perfect for the role—menacing but funny, too. I especially loved watching Alaina act and sing. She always projected her voice and said her lines with lots of expression.

Sometimes I wandered backstage to watch Sophie and the stage crew, who were painting a big backdrop of Mr. Warbucks's fancy mansion. Other crew members were organizing props and making costumes. I soaked everything up, like *naan* bread sopping up curry. It was hard to believe that all these parts and pieces would ever come together into one smooth show.

One afternoon, during a break, I found myself sitting next to Alaina. She turned to me and said, "Hey, I'm Alaina."

"I know," I said shyly. "I'm Kavi."

"You're the girl who made the commercial for your grandma's cookies, right?" Alaina asked. "I saw it online."

"Oh!" I said, surprised. "I mean, yes."

"It's really good," she said. "I think you sing so well."

"Um, thanks!" I said. Alaina Peterson had seen my commercial! I was floating like a bird in a blue sky.

"I'd love to taste your grandmother's cookies," she said. "See? Your commercial worked!" And when Ms. Tucker called her to the stage for the next scene, Alaina walked away singing, "I love these cookies, these crispy, chewy cookies!"

She was singing *my* jingle! Right then, I felt bad for every not-so-nice thought I'd had about Alaina and her dog, Finley. Even though I still felt a bit jealous that she was playing Annie, I decided that I'd bring Alaina cookies the very next day. I hoped that wouldn't make me seem desperate to be her friend.

The next day at rehearsal, Alaina looked delighted when I handed her a little box of cookies. Later, as we were all working on the orphans' song, she said quietly to me, "Kavi, don't tense up before the high notes. Take a breath and ease into them."

I hadn't realized that I was tensing up. "Thank you so much," I said, grateful for the tip. I tried it. It was a little like yoga: focusing on my breathing kept me from tensing up and improved my singing. I realized I could learn a lot from Alaina.

During the fourth week of rehearsals, there was a big math test. I'd made flash cards to study the formulas, as Ms.

González had recommended. I thought I was pretty well prepared, but the day before the test, Ms. González called me to her office.

"Kavi, Mrs. Roberts and I agree that you should take the math test in my office tomorrow," she said.

"Why?" I asked. "I don't think I need extra time."

"No, but you do need to block out distractions, and this will help," Ms. González explained.

I hesitated, then mumbled, "Taking a test in your office will feel so weird."

"It might at first," Ms. González agreed. "But if you had a physical disability, you'd find a way to do things differently in gym class, right? This is the same thing, so let's give it a try."

I wondered if Mrs. Roberts had told Ms. González that she'd caught me humming in class the other day. I'd been thinking about the show and started humming without realizing it. Mrs. Roberts had tapped on my worksheet with her finger and said, "Kavi, this is math class, not choir."

So on test day, instead of going to my math class, I went to Ms. González's office, carefully avoiding eye contact with anyone I knew.

"Come on in, Kavi," said Ms. González, inviting me to a table in a corner of her office.

After the test was over, as I was leaving, I saw Jake coming out of another office nearby. "Hey," he greeted me. "Math test?"

I nodded. "Ms. González thought I would do better in a private room."

To my surprise, Jake gave me a high-five. "It works for me," he said as we walked back to class.

I got an A-minus on the test, which was even better than I'd expected. Ms. González was right. Not having the distraction of other students had helped me stay focused.

One Saturday evening in the middle of February, Mom turned on the weather report. The meteorologist showed maps of swirling patterns, saying, "Snow and icy conditions will develop overnight. We'll get six to eight inches of snow with this arctic air mass. Stay warm, everyone."

Mom made us hot milky chai and *pakoras*, or spicy fritters. "It's time to get cozy and play board games," she announced.

Outside we could hear the wind howling. Scamper jumped up on the couch and snuggled beside me as we began a game of Scrabble.

Dad called Dadima and asked, "Do you want to be snowed in with us?"

She drove over before the streets got too snowy and hunkered down with us.

In bed that night, from the warmth of my covers, I watched the flakes flutter and fall in the streetlights. Soon snow covered the streets and trees and roofs. There were no cars, and the world seemed amazingly quiet.

The blizzard continued on Sunday. Many neighborhoods, including Dadima's, had lost power from trees falling on power lines. The newscasters warned people to avoid driving on the icy roads, but there were still a lot of accidents. Finally, Mom turned off the TV.

Early Monday morning, Mom got a text from the school. "It's a snow day," she announced. As Rishi and I began a celebratory dance, she said, "Wait—there's more. Sounds like there's been storm damage to a wing of the middle school."

"What?" I asked, my breath caught in my throat. "Which wing?"

The auditorium was an addition to the original school building. It was often called the arts wing.

Mom's eyes scanned the text. "It's the auditorium."

I raced to my phone. Texts were flying from the entire cast and crew. How damaged was the auditorium? Could they fix it in time for the performance? It can't be that bad. They'll fix it in no time. What if they can't?

And the million-dollar question: What would this mean for the show?

After worrying about it for a few hours, I said, "Dad, it's stopped snowing, and the snowplows have come. Could we please drive by the school and see how bad it is?"

Dad agreed. We got in the car, and drove extra slowly along the empty roads. When we turned the corner onto the street where my school was, I gasped. A huge limb of the magnificent oak tree had broken off and fallen onto the roof of the arts wing, which looked partly collapsed. The area around it was roped off.

"Oh, beta, that doesn't look good," said my father, the architect. "That's going to need major repairs."

My heart sank. Suddenly all my disappointment over playing an orphan was forgotten. I thought of how much I loved the songs and how fun it was to be in a show with my friends. What would happen now?

By Tuesday morning, the roads were cleared, the school had its electricity back on, and classes resumed.

When my bus pulled up, I saw that the branches on the roof of the arts wing had already been removed. The area was still roped off and the roof was covered with a huge blue tarp, a reminder of the storm and the damage.

That afternoon, instead of a rehearsal, Ms. Tucker and Miss Clarke called a special cast meeting. Since the auditorium was off-limits and the gym was in use, we gathered in the empty cafeteria.

Ms. Tucker raised her hand to get everyone to stop talking. She began, "First of all, we're all thankful that no one was hurt and the damage to the school was limited to one wing." Then she took a deep breath. "I'm sure all of you are wondering what this means for our production of *Annie*."

All of us started talking over each other, asking questions. Ms. Tucker raised her hand again. "I wish we had answers to all your questions. Once the engineers and inspectors assess the damage and determine how long it'll take to fix, we'll know more. For now, we'll continue with rehearsals, which will be held here in the cafeteria."

We looked around. There was no stage, just an empty area near the back of the room where the tables had been pushed against the wall so the janitors could clean. Rehearsing here would be nothing like being onstage. But I swallowed my disappointment. As long as the stage was fixed by the time the show was ready, everything would be okay.

Soon a rumor that the show itself might be held in the cafeteria was flying around the school.

"That would be terrible," I said to Pari and Sophie at lunch, gesturing at the space around us. "There's no stage, no theater lights, no sound system, not even a curtain!"

"It would be tragic to have the show here," Pari agreed. "It just wouldn't be the same."

Sophie nodded. "I know. I heard that it might be postponed until next year instead."

"What?" This was shocking news. "Why?" I asked.

"Because the roof repairs won't be done until the fall," Sophie said. "At least, that's what Jake told me."

"I sure hope he's wrong about that," I replied, getting up to clear my tray.

"But if he's not, maybe it *would* be better to wait," said Pari. "I mean, I'd rather perform in the auditorium, even if it means waiting until the fall. Wouldn't you?"

It felt like an impossible question. To me, both options were terrible.

The question seemed to haunt that afternoon's rehearsal in the cafeteria. Everyone was on edge, and soon lines were drawn between Team *Annie*-should-go-on and Team *Annie*-should-be-postponed.

Finally Ms. Tucker said, "No more discussion. We are rehearsing now. Everyone, take your places."

As I got up to join the other orphans, Alaina said to me with a wobble in her voice, "I'll be in high school next year. If the show is held in the fall, I won't get to be Annie."

I stopped. How had I not thought of that? If it happened, would there be new auditions in the fall? Would there be a new Annie? I had been the only seventh-grader who tried out, so none of the other girls who had auditioned for the role would be here in the fall. Did that mean I would get the role?

Was that what I wanted?

I shook my head to clear it. It was true that I had been jealous of Alaina at first, but now I was more like her fan— and she was almost a friend. Besides, I knew that she was the best Annie. She had earned the role fair and square, worked very hard on it, and deserved to be Annie in our show. It just wouldn't be right for someone else—even if that someone was me—to play Annie in this production.

I squeezed Alaina's arm. "Don't worry about it right now," I told her, wishing I had something more reassuring to say. "Let's just focus on nailing the orphanage scene."

We took our places and began the first scene, but our singing was lackluster. Even Alaina didn't have the gusto that she normally did. Our show felt like a cake that had collapsed in the middle.

At the end of the rehearsal, as we filed out of the cafeteria, I overheard some kids saying, "Maybe we should just cancel the whole show. What's the point of doing it at all, if we can't do it right?"

Lying in bed that night, I couldn't stop thinking about the rehearsal. *Would* they cancel the show?

The idea of the show being canceled hurt so badly, it felt like a physical pain.

I rolled over and punched my pillow, trying to get comfortable. I'd started the year with such high hopes. Why did there have to be a snowstorm? Why did the tree branch have to fall on the roof and wreck our auditorium? I felt tears sting behind my eyelids, and knew I couldn't sleep. I sat up and reached for my journal.

I wanted to write something important, something to express all the feelings that were thudding through my heart, but all I could think of to say was:

The show must go on. It must!

Obedience Training
Chapter 14

Alaina brought her dog, Finley, to the next rehearsal, which cheered everyone up and gave us something fun to focus on. With her wagging tail, golden cocker spaniel coat, soft brown eyes, and bouncy energy, Finley stole everyone's heart.

"She's so doggone cute," I told Alaina.

But when it came time to act, Finley simply wagged her tail harder when Alaina ordered her to sit or lie down. When Alaina said, "Finley, come!" Finley didn't budge.

Alaina was distracted by Finley's behavior and forgot her lines. After the disastrous scene, Ms. Tucker said, "Let's take ten."

I saw Alaina sitting by herself with Finley and went over.

"Finley didn't do very well, did she?" Alaina said glumly.

"It was her first rehearsal," I said. "She'll do better next time." I stroked Finley's silky fur. "Maybe she just needs some training. Why don't you come over to my house this weekend, and we'll work with her. My brother's very good with animals."

Alaina perked up and smiled. "Finley, did you hear that? We're gonna go see a dog whisperer!"

Saturday morning, Alaina came over with Finley to practice. I kept pinching myself that she was actually at my house.

I had peanut butter and chicken treats ready. Rishi started by throwing a stick. "Fetch," he said to both dogs.

The stick arced high in the air, and both dogs took off after it. The sound of a metal trash can clanging in my neighbor's yard startled us all. Finley stopped, turned, and then bounded toward the noise to investigate. Scamper ignored it and kept running, retrieved the stick, and came back to Rishi.

"Moving on," said Rishi. "Let's work on some basic commands."

Finley wasn't a very good student. By the end of the hour, Rishi had gotten her to sit a few times, but she was hopeless at "stay" and "lie down." Scamper, on the other hand, executed every command perfectly.

Alaina looked over at Scamper, who was munching his well-earned treat. "I remember how well he did in your cookie video," she remarked. "I think Scamper should play Sandy instead of Finley."

My heart skipped a beat. "He did that video in just one take, and he's a quick learner. But Ms. Tucker has already cast Finley, so I think it's too late."

"Maybe," said Alaina. "But the thing is, I'll be so

stressed worrying about whether Finley will do what she's supposed to do that it will affect my performance. I wouldn't want to put the whole production at risk any more than it already is," Alaina added. "Having Scamper play Sandy would take pressure off *me*."

I knew she was right. "Okay," I said. "Let's talk to Ms. Tucker about it on Monday."

At the next rehearsal, Finley wasn't there. As Alaina and I explained the situation to Ms. Tucker, Dadima and Rishi appeared in the cafeteria with Scamper. I thanked them and brought him to meet Ms. Tucker.

"We definitely can't have our lead actor stressed about her dog," Ms. Tucker was saying. She gave Scamper a pat and said, "Okay, show me what you've got, pal."

We began by rehearsing the scene with the policeman, played by Jake, in which Sandy has to run to Annie and prove that he's really Annie's dog. Alaina called, "Here, Scamper!" and he ran to her. She gave him a treat. They rehearsed the scene a few times, and Scamper ran to Alaina every time she called him—even after she started calling him Sandy.

"Looks like we have a winner," said Ms. Tucker. "You are a very good boy, aren't you, Sandy?"

Scamper wagged his tail and grinned at Ms. Tucker.

Now I was more eager than ever for the show to go on.

How many girls can say they've acted in a musical with their dog?!

Then I heard someone mutter, "Why are we rehearsing? We don't even have a theater." Several other cast members began to grumble, too. "Putting on a musical in the cafeteria is dumb," one of them said. Ms. Tucker shot the kids a *be quiet* look.

Suddenly I felt angry. Here we were trying to solve a problem, and they were ready to give up on the whole show. My jaw tightened. I took a slow, deep breath through my nose and blew it out even more slowly through my mouth.

"Kavi," said Miss Clarke, "I notice you're practicing some mindful breathing." Yikes, I hadn't realized anyone was watching me. "That would be great preparation for the next song. Could you lead us?" she said.

I'd done this before in my yoga class, but this was school—and some of the boys had a *no way* look on their face. I decided I wasn't going to let them intimidate me. I went up to the front of the group and sat in a lotus pose.

"Take a deep, deep breath," I said, filling my lungs. "Now let it out very slowly, to a count of ten." There were a few giggles and some exaggerated noisy breathing, but by the third deep inhale and exhale, they'd died down. "Let go of all your worries when you breathe out," I said, just like Seemaji did in yoga class.

"Kavi, we should have you do this more often," said Miss Clarke. "The room feels so much calmer."

Suddenly Sophie raised her hand and said, "When I was breathing, I thought of something. My mom works at the community college, and they have a nice theater. Maybe we could put on our show there."

Ms. Tucker shook her head. "Sophie, it's a good idea, but theaters tend to book up months in advance. I've already reached out to several theaters in the area, and they aren't available. I'll call your mom and ask about this one, but we shouldn't get our hopes up."

It was too late for that. You could have heard a pin drop. I knew the silence meant that the whole cast was hoping for a miracle.

Spring Fling
Chapter 15

few days later, at our Thursday rehearsal, Ms. Tucker announced that the community college auditorium was available. A murmur of hope hummed through the cafeteria.

Ms. Tucker raised her hand. "But—"

We groaned. Why is there always a but?

"It's expensive to rent an auditorium," she told us. "Rehearsal time costs money, the equipment and light rental costs money. And the school has already paid for our costumes and the licensing of the play. There is no school budget for any more expenses. We'd have to raise a considerable amount of money in a very short time."

The murmur of hope grew into a buzz.

Miss Clarke said, "Our dress rehearsal is in three weeks. If we want to reserve the theater, we need to pay for it. That doesn't give us much time to raise five thousand dollars. But I can see you want to try—so think about it this weekend, and bring your fundraising ideas to rehearsal on Monday."

We didn't wait for the weekend. The very next day, which was an unusually warm Friday for early March, the whole cast and crew organized a car wash in the school parking lot after school. We had a steady line of customers, but it took a long time to clean the winter grime and salt off of each car. By the end of the afternoon, we counted up our earnings.

"We made three hundred and twenty dollars. That's not even ten percent of what we need," said Jake, throwing a soggy towel into a bucket of dirty water.

"Maybe we should just accept that we'll be performing in the cafeteria," said Alaina.

I hated to give up, but I had to admit that raising enough money to rent the theater was daunting.

That weekend at the Indian Community Center we were celebrating Holi, a festival to mark the arrival of spring.

"We throw colored powder, so Holi is called the Festival of Colors," Rishi explained to Sophie as she got in the car with us. "The powders are made by mixing corn starch and food dye." Rishi seemed pleased to know more than someone his big sister's age, and Sophie listened attentively.

"I can't wait to see the Bollywood dances," she said.

"Me too," I said. I hadn't been taking dance lessons this winter, and I suddenly felt a bit wistful that I wasn't going to be performing. But I would cheer for Priya's dance group.

When we arrived, Pari came running up with a plate full of brightly colored powders. She greeted us by drawing a yellow streak on my cheeks and then on Sophie's. Joining the festive crowd, we grabbed plates of pink, yellow, and blue powders, and then it was a free-for-all as we tossed the powders at each other's clothes, laughing as clouds of color filled the air. Sophie caught Rishi and colored his stomach blue as he giggled and shrieked. Pari turned my hair bright green. It was like a snowball fight, but with colors. Even Mom and Dad joined the fun.

Sophie took a picture of me. "Your plain white shirt is now rainbow colored."

That gave me an idea. "Hey—maybe we could tie-dye white T-shirts and sell them—"

"To raise money for the theater rental," Sophie said, finishing my thought.

"We should throw a spring fling," said Pari. "Like a Holi festival, but at school!"

At rehearsal on Monday, we couldn't wait to present our idea. As the students gathered, I raised my hand. "Let's have a fair at school, with food and games and activities," I said. "We'll sell cookies and tie-dyed T-shirts inspired by the colors of Holi and spring!"

"We'll call it the Spring Fling," said Pari.

"The Spring Fling," said Ms. Tucker, nodding. "I like that!"

Alaina said, "I'll auction singing lessons to the highest bidder!" Other students began suggesting ideas for activities and things to sell. Face painting, sand art, pots of vegetables and flowers . . . The ideas flowed.

Miss Clarke looked around at our eager, animated faces and said, "I'm so happy that all of you want to perform in a theater so much that you are willing to work hard to make it happen."

Ms. Tucker cleared her throat. "I don't want to be a wet blanket, but we must make a commitment to the community college. I'll call and see if they will give us one more week to pay for the auditorium rental. We can't ask them to wait any longer."

Alaina and some of the eighth-graders made a snippet of all of us singing songs from the show to post on the school's website. I helped write the post. It said:

The show must go on! The storm damage to our school and the hard knocks of life aren't stopping us from dreaming about tomorrow. We're raising money to rent an auditorium, and you can help us by coming to the Spring Fling this weekend and spending generously. There'll be games and food and fun! Don't miss out!

The next day after school, Sophie, Pari, and I met at Pari's house to make our Holi-inspired tie-dyed T-shirts. Our parents had generously donated the money to buy supplies, and I had made a list of supplies with a check mark by each: cotton T-shirts, rubber bands, fabric dyes, and plastic buckets to hold the dye. Pari had organized it all in her garage.

"Production starts now!" declared Sophie in a theatrical voice.

I did a drum roll on the lid of the garbage can.

Pari called, "Ready, set, dye!"

We made three dozen T-shirts in different sizes. We rigged up a drying line and hung them all up. It looked

like a rainbow had exploded in Pari's garage.

The rest of that week was a blur of rehearsals and homework and getting ready for the Spring Fling. On Friday after school, Pari and Sophie came over to help decorate cookies. Dadima had made dozens of sugar cookies, and we decorated them using colored sugar and icing. When we were finished, the cookies looked like they'd been to a Holi festival.

Sophie snapped a photo. Her picture made it look like the cookies stretched from here to infinity. Pari sent the photo to all her groups, adding, "Come get some cookies at the Spring Fling tomorrow. All proceeds go toward the middle school production of *Annie!*"

I added, "You know you want one!"

Saturday arrived, a perfect spring day. There was one cloud in the sky, shaped like a flower. Was it a cumulus? I wasn't sure. But who cared, as long as it didn't rain on our Spring Fling!

The fair was set up in the school parking lot. Pari brought tablecloths for our tables and an easel to display a poster I had made about Holi, so our customers would know that our colorful cookies and T-shirts were inspired by the Festival of Colors. Sophie and I piled the boxes of cookies and the stacks of T-shirts in our booth. We were ready to raise some big bucks!

The Spring Fling was well attended, and by the end of the afternoon, we were completely sold out of cookies and T-shirts. Pari, Sophie, and I were exhausted, but elated.

"Do you think we raised enough money to rent the college theater?" asked Pari.

"It seems like we made a lot," I said. "We'll find out on Monday whether it was enough."

On Monday after school, we joined the rest of the *Annie* cast and crew in the cafeteria. As soon as Ms. Tucker and Miss Clarke came in, Jake burst out, "How much did we make?"

Ms. Tucker said, "You raised two thousand, nine hundred and seventy-five dollars. That is an incredible amount to raise on very short notice." She paused and cleared her throat, then added, "I know how hard you all worked. And we received some generous donations."

A hush fell. Even with our car wash money added in, we all knew it wasn't enough. Nobody spoke.

I thought about all my struggles with my grades this year and my inability to focus—and what a difference it had made to understand myself better and reach out to get the support I needed. If there was one thing I had learned last fall, it was that if people understand that you're struggling, they will usually try to help.

I raised my hand.

Ms. Tucker said, "Yes, Kavi?"

"Have we told the people who run the college theater our story?" I asked. "You know, about the storm damage to our school?"

Ms. Tucker shook her head. "No, I didn't go into all that."

"Maybe we should," I said. "Maybe they would help us if they understood our situation."

Ms. Tucker looked at Miss Clarke. Miss Clarke turned to the cast. "How many of you think we should ask for special consideration?" she asked.

Every single hand shot up.

"What do we have to lose?" said Jake.

Showtime!
Chapter 16

To plead our case to the community college, Ms. Tucker decided Alaina, Sophie, and I should go: Alaina because she was Annie, Sophie because she represented the crew and her mother had been our contact with the college, and me because it was my idea to tell our story. Sophie's mom had set up the meeting, so she met us at her office and invited us in to speak with Mr. Paulson, the facilities manager.

Ms. Tucker introduced each of us and said, "Kavi wants to tell our story and explain our circumstances."

I told him about our school and our very ambitious spring production of *Annie* and what had happened in the winter storm in February. "Mr. Paulson, we've worked so hard on this show, and we've raised a lot of money, but we're about seventeen hundred dollars short of your theater rental fee," I said. "Our show goes on next week, and we'd really, really like to do it in your big theater instead of in our middle school cafeteria."

After hearing us out, Mr. Paulson said he had to talk to his supervisor and the chair of the performing arts department. Then he would let us know.

At the next rehearsal, Ms. Tucker gathered the cast and crew. "Mr. Paulson said he was inspired by all of you," she announced. "He pleaded our case—and the college said we could have until the end of the school year to pay off the rest of the money, and we can perform *Annie* in their theater!"

"YESSSSSSS!!!" I shouted, as Alaina burst into happy tears.

On Friday afternoon, we all piled into a school bus and rode to the college theater for our dress rehearsal. Our excitement could barely be contained inside the bus.

In the big college auditorium, I clutched Sophie's hand as we walked toward the broad stage. The polished wooden floor gleamed. From the stage we surveyed the auditorium, the rows upon rows of plush empty seats. This theater was considerably larger than our middle school auditorium. Would we be able to fill it?

When we started our dress rehearsal, Alaina said she felt dizzy, so Miss Clarke gave her a paper bag to breathe into. I realized that even someone as talented and confident as Alaina could still get stage fright. Everyone had their challenges.

About an hour into the dress rehearsal, Mom arrived with Scamper. He wouldn't stop sniffing in every corner of the unfamiliar stage and didn't follow orders as he usually did. I got so distracted watching and worrying about Scamper that I missed my cue three times.

Somehow, we made it through the whole play, but it was a mess. Scamper was the least of our problems. The lighting and music cues were all off, the blocking didn't fit the new stage, and none of the props were in the right places at the right time. We weren't ready to perform the show tomorrow, and we knew it.

Ms. Tucker's brow was furrowed and her voice hoarse as she called, "Let's take a minute!"

We all stopped in our tracks, like when you pause a video. It was one of the theater games we sometimes played, freezing in position.

"Kavi," she began. Oh, no—was she going to correct me for my missed cues? She spoke quietly. "We need to run through this show again if we're going to be ready for tomorrow night, and I'm losing my voice, so would you lead us all in a relaxation exercise?"

I stepped forward and coached the cast through some deep, focused breathing followed by a few easy asanas, and I felt the tension ebb away like the tide on a beach.

When the second run-through began, something strange happened. I was tired—we all were—but it was as if a new source of energy had opened up inside me. I almost forgot where I was—in fact, I almost forgot *who* I was. As we sang the opening number, I truly felt as if I was an orphan during the Great Depression with no family or hope for a better life. The feeling must have come through in my singing, because when we finished, Miss Clarke and Ms. Tucker whispered together, and then Miss Clarke said, "Kavi, we'll add a microphone on you."

Alaina caught my eye and gave me a thumbs-up. My heart pounded with joy. Maybe I wasn't Annie, but I would get to sing with a microphone! I beamed brighter than a full moon. I couldn't wait to tell Mom and Dad.

The next day, an hour before I had to leave for the theater, Rishi took the other actor in the house for a walk, in preparation for his big night. When they came home, Scamper was a mess. "I let him romp and play in the mud," said Rishi. "He loved it!"

I felt a rush of annoyance and was about to scold Rishi and make him give Scamper a shampoo. Then I realized that Scamper looked exactly like a street dog—which was perfect for the first scene when Sandy meets Annie. The dirt streaks even made his coat look sandy colored. I took a picture of Scamper and sent it to the cast: *Sandy is ready for his debut!*

At five o'clock, Mom and Dad dropped me off for hair and makeup. They would bring Scamper shortly before showtime.

This theater had real dressing rooms, where the cast was buzzing with excitement as we put on our stage makeup and costumes. We orphans all wore shapeless gray dresses. Miss Clarke looked at us and said, "The dresses may be drab, but the shine in your eyes is dazzling!"

Ms. Tucker fastened a curly red wig on Alaina's head. She looked perfect. She struck a pose, and we all cheered.

In the greenroom, several parent volunteers had set out a buffet of sandwiches, chips, fruit, and yogurt cups. But I couldn't eat. Butterflies had found a home in my stomach, and my appetite flew away. I was nervous for myself—and for Scamper. I prayed that he would be the smart, good boy that he always was. I couldn't even think about the possibility of my dog messing up the show.

As curtain time approached, Miss Clarke attached a microphone to Alaina's collar. Then she came over and pinned one on me. I was sure that it would pick up my pounding heart.

When the houselights dimmed and the overture began, Alaina and I peeked out at the audience. There wasn't a single empty seat. Alaina squeezed my hand, and I squeezed back. Then the curtain slid open, revealing a roomful of orphans, and the show began.

In the policeman scene, when Alaina called to Sandy, Scamper bounded to her, just as we'd practiced in our backyard. And when we sang "Tomorrow," Scamper lifted his head and crooned along with us in a mournful howl.

It took us entirely by surprise—he had never done that in rehearsal! The audience broke into applause right in the middle of the song.

After the song was over, we all hugged him while his tail wagged furiously. It's fair to say, Scamper stole the show! Thankfully Jake's dad got it all on video, so when we tell the story of this night for the rest of our lives, we'll have proof.

At the end, the entire cast linked hands and raised them

high and bowed again and again to thundering applause.

After the curtain closed for the last time and our proud families finally left the lobby, the cast all helped to strike the set. I looked around at the empty auditorium and suddenly felt overcome with emotion.

Annie was over. It had been such a huge part of my life for three months. Now that it was finished, my heart ached. Something I loved was gone forever. The feeling was like homesickness, but sharper. I found a quiet place backstage and sat on the floor with my head on my knees and let the tears flow.

When I heard the soft sound of someone approaching, I hurriedly rubbed my tears away.

Alaina knelt down beside me. "I know exactly how you feel. I'm super sad too, even though it was the best night of my life," she said in a wavery voice, putting her arm around me. "Now I can't believe it's over."

After a few more tears, we stood up and hugged one more time. Then we followed our castmates out to the parking lot, where parent volunteers were waiting to take us to the cast party at Jake's house.

At the party, we ate tacos and rehashed the show and all the memorable scenes and hilarious moments, reliving them, again and again.

By the time I went to bed that night, it was long past midnight. My body was worn out, but my heart was overflowing.

Showtime!

Next week was spring break. I made a list of everything I wanted to do:

1. Help Dadima with her cookie business.
   - Compose a new cookie jingle.
   - Ask Priya to shoot a video and post it.
2. Make my room look like one of those super-organized ones on TV shows! (as if)
   - Clean out drawers, fold my clothes, put them back.
   - Donate stuff I've outgrown.
3. Visit Alaina for the voice lessons that Mom and Dad bought for me at the Spring Fling!!!
4. Bring Rishi to Alaina's house to put Finley through doggie boot camp.

Alaina was determined to teach Finley some manners, and I knew if anyone could do it, it was my brother.

Near the end of spring break, at our last voice lesson, Alaina told me about her plans to attend a musical theater summer camp in the Pocono Mountains in Pennsylvania.

"An away camp? For four weeks?" I said. "You're so lucky!" For a moment, I felt the old pang of jealousy creep back, but I reminded myself that Alaina Peterson was no longer my idol and rival—she was my friend.

"I'll send you a link. You should come too!" said Alaina.

"Really? Me?" I asked. Was she serious?

"You're a great dancer, and you have a good voice," Alaina said. "The camp will help you get even better. Then you'll really have a shot at playing a lead role in the spring musical next year."

It sounded amazing. I printed out the camp brochure and fantasized about living and breathing musical theater for a whole month. The next day was Saturday, so when Mom and Dad were nice and relaxed after yoga, I gathered my courage and handed them the brochure without saying a word.

"What's this?" asked Dad.

"A summer camp for musical theater?" said Mom.

"Alaina is going, so I wouldn't be alone," I pointed out, crossing my fingers.

And miraculously, my parents agreed to let me go!

My life was anything but hard knock. In fact, tomorrow looked bright and beautiful.

MEET ARUSHA, a Young Dancer

Like Kavi, Arusha and her family live in New Jersey. Arusha, who is 12, served as an adviser on Kavi's story. Here, she talks about her love of Indian dance.

I have been taking dance lessons for the past eight years, mostly *Bharatanatyam* and Bollywood dance styles. My love for dancing came from my elder sisters, who also dance. I have been part of my dance school's competitive team since 2016.

My favorite dance style is Bollywood because it has introduced me to other dance forms such as ballet, hip-hop, folk, jazz, acrobatics, and many more! Learning this style has helped me connect to both my Indian heritage and culture, especially in helping me understand words in the Hindi language as well as Hindi books, songs, and movies.

I believe that the most challenging part of dancing is synchronization. Especially when there is a dance with so many people in it, it takes a lot of hard work and practice to make the dance look perfect and well-coordinated!

I've had the opportunity to perform in many different places through my dance school. Two of the most memorable places were Universal Studios in Orlando, Florida, and Carnegie Hall in New York City. Once I was chosen to introduce my team's competitive dance by giving a two-minute presentation in Hindi. I practiced the speech, and my mom helped me with my accent. Everything was going smoothly until I realized the number of people coming to the competition—over a thousand people in the audience! The night of the show arrived, and as the curtain rose with the spotlight shining on me, my heart pounded so hard I could feel it in my ears! I heard my family and friends cheering me on, and the butterflies scattered away! I picked up the microphone and delivered the intro with renewed confidence.

When Arusha was 8, she danced a classical Indian style called Bharatanatyam *at her grandparents' 50th anniversary.*

Performing at a Diwali celebration, age 9

The classical Indian dance style I am learning requires a graduation ceremony called an *arangetram*. This performance usually includes around 10 pieces mastered over many years of practice. My sisters did theirs, and I remember how much they had to practice to complete this. I am looking forward to doing the same when I'm ready!

I have been doing yoga every Sunday during my weekly Indian culture class for as long as I can remember. Yoga helps me stay calm in my day-to-day life. Whenever I'm about to take a test, I do *pranayam*, a breathing exercise that helps calm my nerves. This process involves inhaling through one nostril and exhaling through the other. It signifies taking in everything good, and getting rid of all that is bad. Whenever you're upset, it works to feel calmer.

In school, math and science are my favorite subjects. It has been a lifelong dream of mine to work at NASA as an engineer involved with space exploration. My other interests include playing the piano, robotics, reading, and coding. Dancing has helped me in playing piano and vice versa. They both teach me to feel the music!

Arusha wearing henna, age 5, and celebrating Holi with family, age 6

READER QUESTIONS

- Kavi says that the story of *Wicked* is "about using the traits you're born with, for good or for bad. And sometimes good and bad are hard to tell apart." What do you think she means by that?

- Would you like to perform in a musical onstage in front of your school classmates? Why or why not?

- Do you think Kavi had good reasons for deciding to drop out of the revue? If you were in her situation, how would you handle it?

- Kavi's feelings toward Alaina are complicated at first. How would you describe them? Have you ever felt a complicated mix of feelings about someone?

- Kavi and her family celebrate Diwali and Holi. What special holidays do you and your family celebrate? What are some of your favorite holiday traditions?

- Have you ever thought that your brain works differently from other people's? If so, do you find the differences to be helpful or challenging?

- Kavi develops ways to feel more calm and focused when she's feeling anxious or distracted. Do you have any tricks that help you stay calm and focused in school or at home?

ABOUT THE AUTHOR

Varsha Bajaj grew up in Mumbai, India—the heart of Bollywood. As a girl she loved reading as well as acting in children's theater. When Varsha moved to Missouri for graduate school, she was lonely at first in a new country. But she found that America was familiar because of the books she had read and the movies she had seen, and soon she felt right at home. Varsha worked as a psychotherapist counseling children and families. Later she moved to Houston, Texas, where she raised her family and began writing children's books. Like Kavi, Varsha loves Bollywood dance and Broadway musicals. Varsha's daughter acted in musicals in middle school, and Varsha had a dog named Scamper!

ABOUT THE ILLUSTRATOR

Parvati Pillai was born in India and now lives in Finland. She is passionate about food, storytelling, travel, and gardening. When she is not exploring the beautiful outdoors, she enjoys experimenting with new illustration styles. Parvati seeks to evoke emotions through colors and hopes that her work brings a smile to people's faces. Follow her on Instagram at @parvatipillai.

ABOUT THE ADVISORY BOARD

Rae Jacobson has a graduate degree in counseling psychology. A native New Yorker, Rae is the the senior writer at the Child Mind Institute. She also writes about mental health, ADHD, and learning differences for *Parenting, New York* magazine, and many other national publications.

Masum Momaya supports artists, activists, scholars, and storytellers working for social justice—especially women, people of color, and people with disabilities—as a curator, writer, coach, and philanthropic foundation strategist. She curated a Smithsonian exhibition, *Beyond Bollywood: Indian Americans Shape the Nation,* which traveled around the United States and India.

Rina Shah is the founder, director, and lead choreographer of AUM Dance Creations, New Jersey's leading dance school. She is trained in Indian classical and Bollywood dance as well as ballet, tap, jazz, and hip-hop. Born and raised in New Jersey, Rina teaches young dancers, produces dance shows, and trains competitive dance teams. She loves traveling with her dancers to spread the art of Indian dance.

Deanna Singh is founder and chief change agent of Flying Elephant, a social impact organization with a mission of shifting power to marginalized communities. An award-winning author, educator, business leader, and social justice champion, Deanna inspires others to build or break systems to create positive change.

Nina Trevens is cofounder and producing artistic director of TADA! Youth Theater, which provides kids from varied social, racial, and cultural backgrounds with original musical productions, musical theater training, and in-school residencies. Many TADA! members and alumni have careers on Broadway and in TV and film.

Allison Tyler is a counselor and social worker who provides strategies and tools for children, adolescents, and families to thrive. A writer and mental health advocate, she works collaboratively with schools, professionals, and the medical community to promote better understanding of ADHD.

Arusha was born in the United States and has taken classical Indian and Bollywood dance lessons since she was five years old. Now she's twelve and still studying Indian dance. Like Kavi, she enjoys participating in family celebrations and loves to give back to the community.

Anna is fifteen and has a particular interest in raising awareness and understanding of mental health and wellness issues, especially those that impact children and school performance.